I0545452

Born to be Bad

LAWRENCE BLOCK
writing as Sheldon Lord

CLASSIC EROTICA

21 Gay Street
Candy
Gigolo Johnny Wells
April North
Carla
A Strange Kind of Love
Campus Tramp
Community of Women
Born to be Bad
College for Sinners
Of Shame and Joy
A Woman Must Love
The Adulterers
The Twisted Ones
High School Sex Club
I Sell Love
69 Barrow Street
Four Lives at the Crossroads
Circle of Sinners
A Girl Called Honey
Sin Hellcat
So Willing

This is for
STEVE AND LETITIA

CLASSIC EROTICA #9

BORN TO BE BAD

Lawrence Block

CHAPTER 1

Only the very rich and the very poor live on the waterfront. Only the very rich and the very poor can vie for the privilege of looking out through their windows at a broad expanse of river or ocean. There are no in-betweens where the water meets the land.

In Florida the waterfront property couldn't be worth more money if the grains of sand were flecks of gold. Between Miami Beach and North Miami Beach there is a stretch of land called Golden Beach where every home is a palace and the ocean is a private moat for each palace, a moat stocked with barracuda instead of alligators but a moat nevertheless.

And in Florida, in Miami, Cuban children dive off the Flagler Street docks and pestilence breeds between the piers on the south shore.

To the north, all that glitters is probably gold. To the North, all the way up the coast to West Palm Beach the sand stretches unimpaired and rich men and women bake brown bodies under the hottest sun in the United States. Waterfront motels collect $25 a day and up for a room, with meals extra. High-class hustlers collect $100 and up for a quick mink-robed roll in the hay.

Around the Flagler Street docks, a room in a flop runs 75¢, a pile of newspapers on a flophouse floor costs a quarter. Around the Flagler Street docks only the bodies of the Cuban children are brown, because a native of Florida knows enough to stay out of the burning rays of the Florida sun.

Around the Flagler Street docks, sex goes for one or two bucks a roll. But the roll is as likely to take place in an alley as in a bed, and signs taped to urinal walls advertise local remedies and local doctors for syphilis and gonorrhea.

It is the same in New York, where Riverside Drive and the Lower East Side stand at opposite poles on the social scale, where Sutton Place and Hell's Kitchen have nothing in common but the water they touch upon.

It's a short haul from Flagler Street to Golden Beach. It's a short swim upstream from a one-room hovel to a twenty-four room castle.

It's a hell of a rough swim.

Rita Morales lived with her mother, three brothers, and four sisters. Rita Morales lived in a single room in a waterfront wooden frame building that would have been condemned years ago if the landlord didn't hand the building inspector a few hundred bucks twice a year, and eight members of her family shared the room with her.

Rita Morales didn't know who her father was. Rita's mother wasn't too sure either, but she did know that there was a good chance that no two of her eight kids had the same father.

Rita Morales was fifteen; she could pass for eighteen with very little trouble. Children grew up quickly down on Flagler Street.

Rita's mother Carmen was 32 and looked 40. Children grew quickly, but women aged even more quickly.

And this was bad.

Because Rita's mother Carmen was growing old, and the men did not want to make love to women who were old. Carmen Morales sat thinking of this, sitting alone in the room with her children outside and the room mercifully quiet.

The children were in school. Or at least the children were supposed to be in school, and if they were not it was little concern to Carmen Morales. If the children would rather dive from the docks or sit in the restaurants listening to the music and sipping the coca-colas, what did it matter to Carmen Morales?

And if the man from the board of education came around again, what did even that matter to Carmen Morales? She would smile at the man, and she would assure the man in rapid-fire Spanish that she did not speak English, and she would smile at the man and convince him that from now on the children would go every day to school, and the man would go away and leave her alone in her room. Perhaps the man would want to feel her a little with his hands the way the last one had, but that was no trouble either for Carmen Morales.

Carmen Morales lifted the skirt of her print dress in her hands and gazed at her legs. They were still good legs, she decided happily. They were still long, and still fairly slender and fairly well rounded. She thought of her neighbor, Dolores Romero, and remembered sadly the way the varicose veins stood out on Dolores' legs. That was bad, those veins that bulged from the side of a woman's legs and made her legs look fat and swollen and old.

Carmen Morales sighed, remembering the days that didn't seem so long ago when she and Dolores Romero had come over from Havana on a boat in the middle of the night. She remembered the boat docking and the *Norteamericano* telling the girls to for Christ's sake be quiet, and she remembered slipping out and being on dry land again.

And then there had been the house. And if living in the house was not so wonderful as the night when Pedro Cadron had made a woman of her for the first time, still it was good. She and Dolores Romero had worn silk dresses and silk stockings, and she could still remember the way her perfume had smelled and how nice her body had felt between the clean white sheets in the house.

But she had not remained that long in the house. Soon she knew that she was going to have a baby. And at 17 she left the house and went to live near the docks on Flagler Street, and when she needed money she walked the streets until she found a man.

At first she took whatever the man gave her. Then she learned more about the business and asked ten dollars, and there were years when she got the ten dollars with no difficulty.

The first baby she named Rita. The second was a boy, and she called him Pedro after her first lover. Then came Rosa and Lola and Esteban and Maria and Carlo and Delia. Eight of them in all, and each one meant more men that Carmen Morales had to seek out and bargain with and finally lead back to the little room in the waterfront frame building.

Carmen Morales sighed softly, hoping that another baby was not on the way. Her time was supposed to begin today; she hoped she was only late and not ready to bear another child. Her price was no longer ten dollars. It had dropped bit by bit, year by year, until now Carmen Morales asked for two dollars and was satisfied to get one. Another baby would mean another mouth to feed and more men to make love with each day, and besides it would mean another few months when she would be unable to work, her belly swelled up with a child.

Although it was strange, but some of the men would pay more for a woman who was expecting a baby. Carmen Morales thought about these men, these men who made her take off her clothes and then caressed her stomach with itching hands and an evil light in their eyes. She did not like these men, but these men would pay money and she needed money.

Carmen Morales leaned back in the chair and thought of Rita. That was a good one, Rita. Young and fiery, and if her tongue sometimes was too hot it was in keeping that a beautiful girl should be spirited. She thought for a moment, considering whether it was good or not that Rita was so beautiful. She would have trouble with the men, of course, and Carmen thought to herself that she would have to tell Rita about men, how to tell a good man from a bad man and how to keep herself for the good ones.

Had Rita kept herself so far? It would be surprising if she had, for already she had seen how the men's eyes followed Rita when she walked down the street, the dozens of pairs of eyes travelling the length of Rita's long, full body.

It was obvious that Rita Morales was Carmen's daughter. One looking now might not see the resemblance, but when Carmen Morales remembers her own beauty that was now gone except for her own memory of it, she could compare herself to her oldest daughter.

The legs were the same, long and rounded and light brown. The breasts were the same, full and proud and jutting forth from a full chest. The hips, too—built for making love and bearing children. And the eyes—wide and deep brown and full of life.

Even the tongue, Carmen Morales thought sadly, remembering Rita's voice cursing at her and telling her to mind her own goddamned business about what time she came in at night.

But wasn't it Carmen Morales' business? Didn't she have to make sure that her daughter stayed pure and good, pure so that a good man would want her and would marry her? Carmen Morales let her mind wander for a moment over the life that might have been hers if she had stayed pure herself and had waited for a man to ask her. A house of her own she might have had, a house of her own and one man to love her and a yard for her children to play in.

Then she remembered the first time, with Pedro Cadron holding her in his arms and telling her how beautiful she was. His hand slipped so gently under her dress and crept over her thighs, sending a new and delicious feeling through her whole body. He opened her blouse, his other hand boldly exploring beneath the folds of the blouse and caressing her firm breasts.

She remembered his mouth seeking the nipples of her breasts, remembered his hard body moving over hers and forcing her, remembered the harsh stab of pain surmounted by the sharp thrill of discovery and rhythm and, finally, overwhelming ecstasy.

And then she had held Pedro in her arms, held him tight against her and lost in the beauty of what had happened. All at once the whole world was peaceful. All at once she could not smell the cooking odors of the kitchen and could not hear the creaking of the bed springs as they strained in a tired mockery of the rhythm of love.

All at once everything was peace and quiet and there was no one in all of Havana but herself and Pedro Cadron.

But had it been worth it? Carmen Morales did not know. It had never been the same after, she knew. No man had ever made her feel the way Pedro Cadron had. If she could have had Pedro and still have remained pure, if she could have let Pedro make love to her on the creaking bed and still have married some respectable man, then everything would have been quite perfect. But it had to be one or the other, and Carmen Morales regretted her choice just as thoroughly as she wished a better life for her daughter.

Rita would not be a whore, a *puta*.

Carmen Morales let her eyes close once again. Outside a boat whistle blew twice—two short, loud blasts followed by silence. Then the silence stopped and she could hear the noises of the street once again, the intermittent cursing in Spanish and English, the rolling of tin cans and beer bottles in the alley by the doorway, the noises of children playing ball in the street with a broomstick for a bat and a manhole cover for home plate.

Soon Rita would be home, followed by the other children. Soon there would be a supper of *paella* to cook and dishes for the little ones to wash. Then there would be streets to walk until Carmen Morales found enough men to buy the food for the next day and pay the rent for the next week.

But until then . . . until then it was very peaceful, sitting in the chair with her eyes shut and her mind wandering back to the happy days in Cuba before the house in Miami, before the trip from Havana, before even the first time with Pedro.

•   •   •

It was that very afternoon that Rita Morales discovered that school was a total and complete waste of time.

The discovery didn't burst in upon her from the blue. She had suspected as much for some time, but that afternoon she decided it once and for all.

It was a waste of time.

She was sitting by the window, trying hard to keep her eyes on what Old Lady Simpkins was writing on the blackboard. But her eyes kept dragging themselves back to the window, and no matter how much Miss Simpkins sweated over logarithms, Rita just couldn't help staring out the window.

It wasn't that she expected to find anything especially exciting out there. God knows it was just another dull street outside with a parade of sweating people and smoking cars and trucks rolling by.

But it was sure as hell more exciting than Old Lady Simpkins and her logarithms.

"Feliz?" Miss Simpkins was giving Feliz Lopez a hard time now. Rita felt sorry for Feliz—he was so stupid, and as if it wasn't enough that he could barely spell his own name, he was also the homeliest boy in the class. Feliz had a face dotted with pimples, and his skin barely covered his thin, bony frame. Everybody picked on Feliz, and Rita wished idly that Miss Simpkins would leave the poor kid alone.

What did it matter whether or not Feliz learned logarithms? If he got lucky he'd wind up driving a pickup truck somewhere in the city, and if he didn't get lucky he'd sweep somebody's floor for the rest of his life for $40 a week.

Nobody needed intermediate algebra to drive a truck or push a broom.

"Feliz, how do you expect to learn this if you don't do your homework? I assign homework every night for a reason. Do you think I get some peculiar enjoyment out of reading your papers?"

Rita turned and gazed out the window. On the street below she saw two men unloading a truck, wheeling racks of cheap cotton dresses into the red-brick warehouse across the street. One of the men pushing the garment rack shoved it over his foot and stopped in his tracks, cursing. Did he know the first thing in the world about intermediate algebra? And was he missing anything?

For that matter, Rita thought suddenly, why should she learn algebra? She was good looking and she was intelligent, so that gave her two possible choices of employment. She could use her beauty to become a whore like her mother or use her brains to become a schoolteacher like Miss Simpkins.

Neither thought was appealing in the least.

She hunched forward at her desk and her sleeveless blouse fell free from her breasts. Rita didn't wear a brassiere if she could possibly help it. It was so damned hot in the daytime, with the sun pounding down from dawn to dusk and the buildings holding the heat in.

Besides, she thought happily, she needed a bra like her mother needed a marriage manual.

Old Lady Simpkins droned on about logarithms and the beauties involved in algebraic computation, but Rita had stopped listening to her several minutes ago. She was smart enough to pass the course with one eye shut anyway, and everybody else in the class was so Godawful stupid that the hour crawled by every day.

Stifling a yawn, she looked out the window again.

And at that moment she decided to stay away from school from then on in.

Outside a Chevy Corvette with the top down was waiting impatiently for a red light to turn green. The car was white with red leather upholstery, but Rita barely noticed the car. There was a man and woman in the car, and they took the whole of her attention.

The man wore a white dinner jacket, a plain bow tie and a matching cummerbund. At that distance it was hard to tell, but Rita estimated his age at 24 or 25. The girl looked younger—18 or 19, probably.

The girl wore a formal blue off-the-shoulder affair, and it was far enough off the shoulder so that from where she sat Rita could examine the girl from her forehead to her waist. Her examination revealed that the girl, when you came right down to it, possessed virtually nothing that Rita herself did not possess in equally impressive quantity.

I've got more than she does, Rita thought. *And my hair is darker and longer than hers, and my complexion is as good and my face as pretty . . .*

For one second she wondered whether the girl in the Corvette knew anything about logarithms.

Then she realized that it didn't matter, and that she could sit in a Corvette herself someday.

And that whether she did or not certainly didn't depend upon her mastery of intermediate algebra.

•   •   •

The class ended, finally. The rest of the students poured out of the classroom in a rush, but Rita instead headed straight for Miss Simpkins.

"I'm leaving," she told the teacher, simply.

"What?"

"I'm leaving."

"That seems sensible. The class is over—"

"You don't understand," Rita said. "I mean I'm leaving school. I'm not coming back."

"You can't."

"You mean because I'm not 16 yet? Nobody cares about that. The truant officer will come down and bother Mom for awhile, but they can't make me go back. They never can."

Miss Simpkins shook her head wearily. "That's not what I meant, Rita. What will you do if you leave now? You know you're the best student in the school. You're the only one I have any hope for, the only one who might be able to turn into something."

"I'll turn into something," Rita cut in.

Miss Simpkins didn't appear to have heard the interruption. "You could teach these children something. The ones that come after you—you could give them an education so that they—"

"So that they can keep books when they push numbers on the street corner?"

Miss Simpkins stopped for a minute, letting her eyelids fall shut. "Maybe that's all I've been doing," she said slowly.

"I didn't mean that—"

"It's all right, Rita. Maybe you're right; most of the others won't turn out any better than they are right now. But a teacher has to live for the few, the gifted ones. Like you."

"Like me?" Rita felt a blush beginning to spread over her face.

"Like you. Rita, do you know how many feeble-minded idiots I have to shout at in order to find one child who understands what I'm talking about? Do you know what an unbearable aggravation it is?"

Rita didn't say anything.

"I want you to be something," the teacher continued. "If the few like you don't turn into something important, something good, then there is no excuse for my entire life. But if a girl like you goes to college and then gets to a higher station in life, if a boy like Mickey Izquelda finally gets to med school and becomes a doctor—Rita, when something like that happens, then everything makes sense again.

"Do you see what I mean?"

"I see."

"Then stay," Miss Simpkins said. "Don't quit—don't be a quitter. I'll give you extra work if the classes are boring. I'll talk to some of your other teachers. There's no point in your wasting time on material that's too easy for you. I'll ask Mr.—"

"Miss Simpkins."

"—Leibowitz if there isn't some way to give you advanced physics instead of the primary—"

"Miss Simpkins—wait a minute."

The teacher paused.

'Miss Simpkins, I'm not coming back. I'm leaving, and nobody can change my mind."

"What are you going to do?"

Rita considered the question. "I'm going to make money," she said. "I'm going to get away from Flagler Street and the waterfront and the docks. I'm going to go someplace where I'll have a house to live in and a car to ride in and good food three times a day and—"

"You little fool!"

Rita stopped. The teacher's words were like a slap in the face.

"You let some . . . some pimp talk you into parlaying your body into a gold mine, didn't you? Do you know how you'll wind up if you do that?"

"I'm not going to be a whore, Miss Simpkins. My mother is a whore, and I'm not going to do that."

"Then—"

"I'm not sure. But I'll find a way, and I won't find it in Miami."

"Where then?"

"I don't know," the girl said. "Maybe New York. Somewhere, anyhow."

"What will you do?"

"Get a job."

"Doing what? My God, you're 15 years old, you're Cuban, you're—"

"I look 18 and I speak perfect English. My Spanish doesn't even sound Cuban. I speak perfect Castilian."

"I know you do. But—"

"I'm going, Miss Simpkins."

The teacher studied Rita's face. There was a hint of unbridled determination in the firm, pointed chin, a set to the mouth that almost convinced her that the girl could do what she said she could.

"Be very careful," she said. "You want to set the world on fire, Rita. Be careful."

"I'm always careful."

Miss Simpkins smiled. "I guess you are," she said. "I hope you change your mind and stay."

"I won't."

"I know you won't. You never change your mind, do you? But why do you tell me all this? I'll only have to report you and make more trouble. You should have gone without saying anything to me."

Rita's eyes were suddenly very serious and very intense. "You won't report me," she said. "I know you won't, because you know it wouldn't do any good and because you wouldn't want to make trouble.

"And I told you because I like you," she added.

They were both silent for a moment, and then Miss Simpkins said, "I like you too, Rita. Good luck."

Rita hurried from the room, down the stairs and out the door to the street. There were dirty words scrawled on the walk and sidewalks, and the alleyway next to the school was littered with empty wine bottles and used contraceptives.

But Rita didn't notice these things. Her mind was filled with visions of Corvette convertibles and handsome men in white dinner jackets, visions of off-the-shoulder formals and a purse full of money and everything she wanted.

On her way home, a slightly drunken sailor lurched toward her, placed one hand on her shoulder and asked her how much she would charge him to let him sleep with her.

Rita turned and regarded him for a long moment with her wide brown eyes.

Then she spat full in his face, turned away, and hurried home with long, purposeful steps.

CHAPTER 2

"I'm going to New York," Rita told her mother.

Carmen Morales looked at her daughter. She was never sure quite how to cope with the girl, feeling always that she ought to be able to help her along, that this was her responsibility. But at the same time there was the ever present feeling that Rita was always a good two steps ahead of her.

"Why?" she asked simply.

"I want to get away from Miami. I want to be somebody, Mom."

"You can't be somebody here?"

Rita shook her head.

"What I want—this does not matter?"

Rita hesitated for a second, then shook her head more adamantly than before.

Carmen Morales lowered her eyes. "*Asi es la vida*," she said. "I—I didn't care for my mother, either. Such is life, eh?"

Rita shrugged, feeling vaguely uncomfortable.

"Perhaps it is best," Carmen Morales went on. "The old, *los vijos*—they grow the children, and when the children are old enough, they leave."

"I have to go."

"I understand. And when you have to do something, you do it. *Verdad?*"

"Yes, that's right."

"*Sí.* You are like me, Rita. Like your mother, and this is both good and bad. Nothing will ever stand in your way, Rita."

Rita was silent.

"But you must be careful. I let nothing stand in my way, and I am still a young woman. But I am a *puta*, and I will be a *puta* until I die. I am 32 and already my breasts sag and my back aches when the rain comes. You—you are smarter than I was. When a man gives you talk that is sweet, tell him to go away. Spit on him."

Rita grinned inwardly, remembering the sailor.

"You understand?"

"I understand, Mom."

"You should call me *Mama*," Carmen Morales complained. "You are not so much the American that you cannot call me *Mama*."

"I—"

"But it does not matter. *Que me importa?* What difference does it make to me, if you are going away to Nueva York and I will not see you any more? How are you going?"

"On the bus."

"The bus. How are you going to pay for the bus?"

"I don't know," Rita said. "It costs $35.64."

"$35.64. And you will have to eat on the way, so it will be $40 at least. And how will you live when you get there?"

Rita shrugged.

"$40," Carmen Morales repeated. "Where are you going to get that much money?"

"Will you give it to me? I'll pay you back."

"When? When you are rich?"

"As soon as I have it."

Carmen Morales drew herself up to her full height. She stood several inches taller than her daughter, and she stared down at her loftily. "I will not give you a penny," she said. "I could say that I do not have $40, but I do have $40. But you cannot have it."

"Why not?"

"Because if you want to go by yourself you shall go by yourself. You shall go owing me nothing, and if you do become rich you shall give me back nothing. Do you understand?"

Rita didn't answer.

"You'll get to New York," Carmen Morales went on. "If you really want to do something you shall do it. You will do it by yourself, and I will not help you. And you never shall have to do anything for me, not even after I am gone."

"When you're dead," Rita said levelly, "I won't so much as piss on your grave."

"That is as it should be," Carmen Morales said. "My bones will rot without your water, and you will get to New York without my money. Now kiss me goodbye and leave."

After the girl had left, Carmen Morales sank wearily into her chair. Suddenly she felt very old, very old and very tired.

In every slum there is a man like Pardo. In every slum there is a man who is tough enough and sharp enough to make money but neither tough enough nor sharp enough to get out of the slum he was born in.

In Harlem this man deals in numbers. In Hell's Kitchen he runs a shoplifting gang and on the East Side he fences stolen cartons of cigarettes. He drives a Cadillac and flashes a roll, but he never gets out of the level he started from. He becomes a *smooth operator*, a man girls are warned against and boys admire.

Pardo was this sort of man.

Pardo's full name was Luis Felipe Pardo, but no one had called him anything but Pardo in years. He was pushing thirty, a fairly tall, slim Cuban with a pencil-line black moustache and greasy black hair that hugged his skull. Pardo dressed so well that he managed to look cheap—his shoes were yellow calfskin and cost $35 a pair, his pegged flannel slacks cost $25 a pair, his shirts were black silk and his sport jackets were imported and cost anywhere from $100 apiece on up.

But Pardo looked cheap and Pardo would always look cheap— cheap and flashy. A quiet man in a $35 charcoal suit would always be a cut above Pardo, no matter how high a polish Pardo's shoes had or how shiny his teeth were or how far the fins of his powder-blue Cadillac extended from the body of the car.

But when a man wanted money, he could see Pardo. Pardo sold marijuana all over the neighborhood and made about $500 a week on a good week, and Pardo always had money or knew where money could be obtained. Pardo was not the Red Cross, but in time of emergency he might be charitable on a whim.

And if you had something to sell, and if what you had to sell was something Pardo wanted to buy, he could often be persuaded into paying you more than your merchandise was worth.

Pardo got what he wanted. All he had in the world was money, and he was willing to pay for what he wanted.

Rita had something to sell. Rita was beautiful and Rita was bright, but when you came right down to it there was only one thing in the world Rita had to sell and it was located between her long brown legs.

And Pardo wanted it.

Pardo was not precisely the most subtle being in the universe, Rita thought. The most subtle being in the universe wouldn't whistle at a 15-year-old girl, and Pardo did a good deal more than whistle.

Pardo patted her on her round behind whenever he got close enough to her. Pardo had a healthy habit of staring at her breasts and grinning wolfishly, Pardo oftentimes dropped sly hints, like "When are you going to let me get in, honey?" and similar guarded advances.

Rita had something to sell.

And when you had something to sell . . .

Rita found Pardo at Eighth Note, a small, poorly lit nightclub where girls gyrated to a Latin-American beat and where patrons were adjudged old enough to drink if they could get their heads over the bar.

Pardo was sitting in a corner booth by himself. He stirred a rum-coke laconically, banging the ice cubes against the side of the glass and staring into the glass morbidly. She sat down across from him and he looked up, his eyes fixing on her face, then travelling downward and coming to rest on her breasts.

"Nice," he murmured absently.

"Pardo—"

He looked up again, shook his head once to clear it, and smiled easily. "Rita," he said solemnly. "Rita Morales, daughter of Carmen Morales, sister of Rosa and Lola and Esteban and Maria and Carlo and Delia and Pedro Morales. What can I do for you that will get me in the same bed with you?"

He asked, she noticed, as if he had given up hope and was just propositioning her for the sake of appearances. He was in for something of a surprise.

"I need money, Pardo."

"Money?"

"Yes."

He nodded, then lifted his glass and sipped his rum-coke. "Have to cut out drinking these," he said. "Damn coke rots the lining out of your stomach. Want a drink?"

She shook her head.

"You want money, though."

"Yes."

"How much?"

"Fifty dollars."

His eyebrows went up a notch and his teeth flashed. "Fifty bucks? That's a lot of bread, sweetie. You mean fifty *Cubano* or fifty *Norteamericano*?"

"Fifty dollars in American money."

He nodded. "Fifty dollars *Norteamericano*. That's a lot of bread, like I said. You expect me to just give you the money, Rita? After you been holding out on Pardo the way you have?"

"I didn't say that."

He nodded thoughtfully. "Sure you don't want a drink, Rita? Drinking is good for a woman."

She considered. She hadn't drunk before, never anything more than a glass of wine with a meal on occasion. But then there were other things she had never done before that she was going to do tonight. The thought of going to bed with Pardo was not particularly attractive to her, and she tried to imagine what it would be like, his body pressing into hers and him leaning on her and . . .

"One drink," she said.

Pardo smiled. He tossed off the remainder of his rum-coke and waved two fingers in the air. A moment later a short, small-boned waiter appeared with two glasses.

"Cheers," Pardo intoned solemnly. They clinked glasses and Rita sipped her drink, noting that it tasted like coke except that it was slightly worse.

"Like it?"

She shrugged noncommittally.

"To get back to the subject—you want fifty dollars. Fifty iron men. Fifty clams, fifty berries, fifty—"

"Fifty dollars," she said.

"Precisely. But you got to have something that's worth fifty dollars, baby. What have you got that I want?"

She leaned back in her chair. "That depends," she said, trying to speak as seductively as possible. "I've got a maidenhead, Pardo. I've got my virginity. You interested?"

His smile grew so wide that she thought his face would crack. "I might be. You want fifty bucks for it?"

"That's right."

"You ought to bargain more. Hell, I know guys pay one, two, three hundred for a virgin."

"All I want is fifty," she said.

"You don't want more if you could get more?"

"No."

"Why not?"

"Because I'm not a whore."

He laughed, the laughter sounding unreal in the smoky night-club. "Then what the hell are you, little one? A plaster saint? A Santa Maria? You want to be the second virgin to give birth or something?"

"All I want," she said, "is fifty dollars. That's all."

For a few minutes neither of them said anything. She finished her drink while he stared fixedly at her breasts.

"Those all yours?" he demanded suddenly.

She nodded, coloring.

"Hell, it ought to be worth that much just to give them a little hug and a squeeze. They look nice to feel, nice to pet and pinch a little. You think you'd like that?"

She didn't reply.

"Nice," he said again. "Course, I'd do more than that for my fifty dollar's worth. Have to do lots more. Have to touch you just about every place, you know?"

"I know."

"Have to take you to bed," he went on. "Have to keep you there all night. Think you'd like that?"

"I don't know," she answered honestly. She wasn't sure whether she'd enjoy sleeping with Pardo or not. She wondered if his breath was bad, wondered whether he would be gentle with her or whether he'd bruise her and hurt her.

She wondered whether or not he bathed frequently, and then she began to wonder about the act itself, the act that was supposed to make her a woman. The act that, if nothing else, would pay her way out of Miami and away from Pardo and her mother and Miss Simpkins and Flagler Street.

"But you're game?"

"I'm game," she said.

"Then let's go."

He stood up and placed a bill on the table. Then she took his arm and they walked out of the club to his car. He opened the door for her, helped her in, and walked around to the driver's side. As he turned the key in the ignition and started the Cadillac, Rita thought to herself that there was a great gulf between her and the girl in the Corvette at that moment. Pardo's car cost more money, but the man in the white dinner jacket was ahead of him in every other respect, just as the girl in the blue formal was ahead of her and out of her class.

The top of the convertible was down, and Rita let her head rest against the seat so that she could stare up at the stars on the way to Pardo's apartment. Pardo lived in Miami, not in the waterfront slum and yet not in a really good section of town. It was the type of neighborhood where people drift who have money without possessing any of the elements that come with honest money, a neighborhood corresponding to Manhattan's west Nineties off Central Park.

Pardo's apartment was at the top floor of an elevated building. The elevator operator flashed the Cuban a wide smile, and Rita guessed that Pardo was an especially generous tipper. She half-hoped that he wouldn't give her more than the fifty dollars agreed upon. More would make it seem like prostitution; fifty dollars—enough to cover bus fare to New York and food on the way and rent and carfare for the first week in the city—made it seem almost moral.

Unaccustomed as she was to luxury, Rita could still sense that there was something wrong with Pardo's apartment. The furniture and the pictures on the walls seemed consciously designed to impress, as if Pardo himself was trying to be sure that he had class. But Rita didn't have much time to inspect the furnishings; Pardo led her through the apartment to the bedroom without stopping.

"Drink?"

She shook her head and he smiled. "Okay," he said. "So let's skip the preliminaries. Fifty you want, fifty you get. Now take off your clothes."

For the first time since she had made her decision Rita felt reluctant. She was beginning to realize just how much of a bridge she would be crossing, just how major an act she was committing.

"C'mon," Pardo snapped.

Mechanically, Rita's hands went to the buttons of her blouse and opened them. Pardo's eyes found the opening of the blouse and watched as she opened the final button and slipped the blouse over her shoulders.

"Magnificent," he said softly.

Then she took off her skirt, first kicking off her shoes. The thin pair of nylon panties followed the skirt and she stood before him naked, her whole body brown and clear and beautiful. She blushed as his eyes fixed on first one and then another part of her, settling first on her breasts, then on her legs and thighs and finally on the dark triangle of hair below her belly.

"Lie down," he commanded hoarsely.

She walked over to the bed and stretched out on her back. He stood over her, gazing at her. Then he sat down on the edge of the bed and smiled.

"Okay," he said. "Now get up and get dressed, Rita. The party's over."

Her eyes widened. "You—"

"I'm not interested," he said. "C'mon, get dressed."

She sat up straight, her eyes blazing with anger. "You promised, damn you! I need that money!"

"What for?"

"That's none of your business. You promised, Pardo!"

His grin widened. "You can have your money, brat. Just give it back to me sometime. I'm not hungry enough to take your sweet little maidenhead away from you just now."

"What do you mean?"

"I mean I'll give you your fifty bucks. Just get dressed and we'll get out of here."

"Don't you want to . . . to—"

"Not bad enough so that it's worth hating myself. Hell, I get enough tail to keep me happy. I don't have to rob cradles with fifty-dollar bills. Just call it a loan."

"No," she said, firmly. "I don't want any loans, Pardo. I don't want to owe you anything. I don't want to be in anybody's debt."

"Why not?"

She didn't answer.

"You think you're better than me?"

"Yes," she said. "I am."

They looked at each other, and suddenly he burst out laughing. "Maybe you are," he said. "Okay, we'll play it your way."

Pardo reached for her and one of his large hands encircled her left breast. His touch shook her and for a moment she started to tremble. Then his fingers began to manipulate her breast gently, almost tenderly.

"Nice," he mumbled.

His fingers toyed with her nipple, pinching and hurting her slightly for a moment. Then the nipple hardened under his touch and a vaguely pleasant feeling began to course through her body.

His other hand found her other breast. His hands worked gently, rhythmically, and she felt a faint thrill of desire building up within her. Her whole body seemed to glow with new life.

His touch was soft, his hands sure. Her body began to twist on the bed and she moved her hips in rhythm, thrusting her body upward in time to the movement of his hands on her full breasts.

"Pardo," she said softly. Then she repeated his name once again, louder and more insistently.

Than all at once his hands released her and his laugh split the silence of the room. "I told you it might be worth fifty bucks just to hug 'em a little. Well, it was. You can get dressed now, baby. You earned your money. You'll get the fifty and you don't owe me a thing."

Her mouth fell open.

"C'mon," he said. "No debt, no nothing. We're square."

"Don't—" She paused in mid-sentence.

"What's the matter?"

"Don't stop," she said.

"I told you there's no debt. Hell, it was worth the fifty just to see you squirm around like that. You're a hot little bitch, Rita. You'd make one hell of a fine hustler if you wanted."

"Touch me . . . again." Her words came slowly, in a husky voice.

She couldn't understand the feelings that were coursing through her, couldn't understand them and didn't want to understand them. All she wanted was Pardo, Pardo's hands on her breasts, touching her and holding her and making her feel so good, so warm and so beautiful.

"You want to be touched?"

She nodded.

"Maybe you want more than just touching?"

"Yes," she said, hardly recognizing the sound of her own voice.

Pardo stood up. She waited impatiently, moving spasmodically on the bed while he removed his clothing and hung it neatly in the closet. Then he too was naked, first standing before her and then seated once again on the bed beside her.

His hands found her breasts once again and the same feeling shot through her, more intense than before. Then he let one hand drop to her leg, massaging the smooth skin there, his fingers tracing little circles on the inside of her thighs. His hand moved higher and she moaned involuntarily, her whole body hot and hungry for him, aching for him.

He lay down next to her on the bed, his mouth finding hers and his tongue probing her mouth. She noticed that his breath was fresh and that his body was clean and hard against her. He took her in his arms and her arms encircled his body, drawing him into her.

He began to move against her, pressing against her. Then a jet of pure pain shot through her entire body as he took her, pain that made her scream out in an instant of sheer agony.

Then the pain disappeared, eclipsed by a wave of pleasure that completely overwhelmed her. She shot higher and higher, moaning and moving in pure perfect rhythm, higher and higher until she reached the very peak.

And everything was perfectly still.

Chapter 3

When she looked through the window there was nothing but a vast expanse of blue. The clouds were below her, and she thought how strange it was to look down to see clouds. She leaned back in her seat and closed her eyes, relaxed and happy.

Pardo was right; a plane was much more comfortable than a bus. Rita felt a momentary flash of guilt at having permitted Pardo to pay for the plane, but her guilt vanished when she thought more about it.

Because she realized that she didn't feel at all like a prostitute. She had let Pardo make love to her because she wanted him to, and even now she could remember the way the unfamiliar feelings had coursed through her body, the way her skin felt more alive than ever and the way her body slipped so easily into the driving, pulsing motion of primitive lovemaking.

Afterwards Pardo had begged her to stay, to live with him as his mistress. For a moment, lying in his bed with his arms around her, she had almost been willing to accept the life he would have given her.

But the moment had passed.

Instead of fifty dollars for her body, Pardo took her body for nothing and gave her far more than the fifty dollars they had agreed on. First he paid her plane fare. Then he insisted on outfitting her with clothes and luggage, explaining that cheap blouses were all right for Flagler Street but that she would need much more when she tried to make the grade in New York.

And there was extra money generously supplied by Pardo—money for rent, money for subway fare, money for food until she got the big break in New York and landed the job she was looking for.

She thought about Pardo, wondering for a moment whether it might not have been better to stay with him. He had money, he even seemed to love her—but there was something more than love and money that she wanted. She wanted to be somebody, and being the mistress of Luis Felipe Pardo was not enough.

When the plane passed over Golden Beach, Rita looked out of her window to catch a glimpse of the row of millionaire's homes. That, she knew, was what she wanted. A vast expanse of private beach, a cluster of million-dollar homes that she could barely see from the plane.

She closed her eyes again, letting her mind wander and finally drift off to sleep. It seemed only seconds later that the plane was taxiing to a perfect landing at LaGuardia Airport, and she was suddenly in New York.

The advertising in the New York *Times* said there were inexpensive and clean rooms for rent at 147 West 46th Street. She needed a room first of all, right away before she could even begin to think about a place to work or anything of the sort.

The cab ride to the rooming house was an experience. All at once she became aware of the immense size of New York. Miami was a big town, but New York was a city, the biggest city, and the difference was almost incomprehensible. She felt that she had never seen so many people in her native life—people running back and forth, people moving and talking and hurrying from one place to another without coming from anywhere and without appearing to go anywhere.

The cab stopped, but she didn't notice it. And the cabby had to crane his neck over the seat and tell her twice in a loud voice that she was at her destination before she realized what he was talking about. Her mind seemed to be trying to race off in a dozen different directions at once and she could barely think straight.

She paid the cab driver, tipping him a quarter after he helped her carry her two suitcases to the door of a rather rundown building. He opened the door for her and she lugged the suitcases inside, setting them down in front of the desk and smiling hesitantly at the tired looking woman behind the desk. She shifted from one foot to the other, waiting for the woman to speak.

"You looking for a room?" The woman's voice was faded and grey, just as the woman was. She seemed to be a person who had given up, an old woman living her life out and waiting to die. For a moment Rita thought she resembled her mother, but she saw in another second that the only point of resemblance was the wasted-out quality in the woman's eyes, the almost dead nature of her face.

"Yes," Rita began. "I saw your ad . . ."

"Ten dollars," the woman said. "Ten bucks a week, the first week in advance. And no men in your room. I don't care what hours you keep or what you do so long as you don't do it here. Okay?"

"I'd like to see the room first."

The woman turned around in her chair and took a key from a peg on the wall. She placed it on the desk and gave it a slight push in Rita's direction.

"Third floor up," she said. "I'd go with you but I'm too tired. You go up and take a look at it and come straight down."

Rita fought off an impulse to tell the woman what she could do with her room and picked up her suitcases. The second flight of stairs seemed a good deal steeper than the first and she was out of breath by the time she reached the top landing. She found her room quickly enough—there were only two in all on the third floor—and fitted the key in the lock.

The room was pleasant enough. Just the idea of having a room all to herself made it a big change from Flagler Street, and the rundown bed and shabby dresser didn't disturb her. She stretched out on the bed for a moment, making sure that it was comfortable, and opened the drawers of the dresser to be sure the room wasn't too filthy. It seemed all right, and she was in no mood to be fussy.

"I'll take it," she told the woman when she had returned to the first floor again. She handed the woman two crisp ten dollar bills and the woman pushed a register and pen at her.

Rita hesitated only for a second; then she signed the register *Rita Martin.*

The woman reclaimed the book and examined the signature carefully. "That your real name?" she demanded.

"Of course. Why?"

The woman's face relaxed into a slow smile. "Took you for a Puerto Rican," she explained, handing Rita four dollars in change.

"Room'll only cost you eight a week now. Landlord told me to push up the price for them Spics."

Rita swallowed, alternately glad she had the foresight to use a false name and furious with the woman, aching to reach out and wring her bony neck.

"I'm not," she said.

"Yeah," the woman said. "Yeah, I noticed you speak good English and all. Well, you make mistakes in this business." She grinned to show that she had meant no insult, and Rita forced a grin in reply to hide the fact that the woman had indeed insulted her.

Back in her room, the first thing she did was unpack her clothes and put them away in the dresser. Then, her unpacking finished and her suitcases closed and stored in the closet, she sat down on the bed to take stock of herself.

The room wasn't at all bad. The one window at the far end provided her an exciting view of the brick wall of another building, and the ceiling was low and the floor dirty, but otherwise she was as comfortable there as she would have been anywhere else.

But where did she go from here? She picked up the copy of the *Times* where she had seen the room advertised and hunted for the job listings. She scanned them rapidly, looking for something that would be right for her.

There didn't seem to be much. All the jobs called for experience—either that or they were simple, menial things like filing or typing that didn't interest her in the least. There was no point in coming all the way to New York to get a menial job in an office for $40 a week. It didn't make sense, not at all.

She went through the listings a second time, then angrily

balled up the paper and threw it against the wall. Flinging herself down on the bed, she wondered why she had come to New York at all, why she didn't have the brains to stay with Pardo or at least to stay in Miami. What was the point of it all?

It seemed so sensible when she was back on Flagler Street. It seemed so easy—you just get on a bus and get to New York and make your fortune. But there didn't seem to be any place to start. A room in New York wasn't much different from a room in Miami or anywhere else, and she didn't have any greater chance of success on West 46th Street than any other place in the world.

Suddenly her skin felt grimy from the trip and she decided a shower would be in order. The woman had mentioned a bathroom down the hall, and she hauled herself off the bed and began stripping down.

She hung her skirt and sweater in the closet, slipped off her shoes and slipped into a pair of bedroom slippers Pardo had provided. Then she pulled the silk panties down over her hips, giggling at the way the silk slid luxuriously over her smooth skin.

The silk panties had been Pardo's idea. "One pair for each day of the week," he had insisted. "Black for Saturday because that's the sexiest and you'll be going out on Saturday night. Even if nobody's going to get a look at your pants you ought to at least feel sexy.

"White for Sunday because it's pure. Blue for Monday, green for Tuesday, red for Wednesday, yellow for Thursday, and orange for Friday."

"But what does it matter?" she had asked.

"What does it matter? These panties cover my favorite part of you, and I want that part well covered. No cotton for you, Rita. No rayon either. Silk!"

And silk it was. But Rita had drawn the line when Pardo tried to buy her a brassiere. What in the world did she need one of those things for? When she got old, when she began to droop—that would be time enough. But for the time being she would go about without her breasts bound up like the feet of a Chinese woman. The one bra she had owned now reposed graciously in a Flagler Street trashcan, and it was much better that way.

She stretched out on the bed, naked except for the bedroom slippers on her feet. Her hands reached up and cupped her breasts, but somehow it was different from the time Pardo had held them in his strong brown hands. Languidly she ran her hands over her body, stroking her firm full thighs and flat stomach.

She thought suddenly how much easier it would be to be a prostitute. She had heard of the New York call girls, women who got fifty or a hundred dollars for spending the night with a man. It was tempting, but she had to aim higher than that.

But, she mused, it would be nice to have a man, a man to make her feel like a woman again. If only a man would come to her now, come right to the door and knock.

She waited, expectantly, for a knock at the door.

There was a knock at the door.

At first Rita thought it was part of her reverie. Then, when the knock was repeated, she was terrified. Up to that point she had been alone; now somebody was coming to her and she had to begin living in a city with people in it. She couldn't be alone, not even here.

"Just a minute," she called. Then she jumped up from the bed, put on her robe and opened the door. The girl at the door was very beautiful. She had the long-stemmed willowy type of beauty, with an oval face framed by long golden hair and a body that had to be called slender despite the high, full breasts and sensuous hips. The girl smiled.

"A new arrival," the girl said. "A new occupant of the 46th Street outhouse. A friend, come to seek her fortune in the cruel and hardened city of New York. I'm Lucia Fallon, friend. Who are you?"

"Rita Martin." She stepped back involuntarily and the girl followed her into the room. "I—"

"Got anything to drink?"

Rita shook her head without answering.

"Hang on a minute," the big girl said. "Be back in a jiffy." She opened the door and disappeared through it, reappearing in a jiffy with a bottle of Dewar's White Label in tow.

"Good Scotch," she said. "Pappy always said never save money on food, whiskey or women. Always buy the best of each."

"I don't have any glasses," Rita stammered. She still wasn't sure precisely what was happening.

"God," Lucia said. "Hang on a minute." She vanished again, then returned with two water tumblers and filled each half full of the Scotch.

"To new arrivals," Lucia said. "To new arrivals and old arrivals and the big break. Right?"

Rita nodded vaguely, and Lucia downed half her drink. in one swallow. Rita sipped hers, prepared to dislike it and was surprised to find she enjoyed it.

"What do you do?" Lucia demanded.

"Do?"

"You know—dance? Sing? Act?"

"Oh," said Rita. "Well—nothing, I guess."

"You work?"

"I'm looking for a job."

"Where are you from?"

"Miami."

"Really? All the way from Florida?"

Rita nodded.

"God! What the hell did you come way up here for? Show biz?"

"I—"

"Just about everybody in this area from out of town is in the business, which is why I asked. We're within walking distance of the agents' offices and the studios, which means no carfare, and when you got no work it makes a difference whether you have to pop a token in the subway turnstile or not. Me, I hoof it in the chorus line. How about you?"

"I don't know," Rita said. "I came up here to get some sort of a job, but I'm not sure what." She decided that she liked Lucia Fallon. She couldn't help admiring the older girl's beauty, and her free and friendly manner was more than pleasant. She sipped more of her Scotch, liking the way the liquid burned a warm path down her throat to her stomach.

"How old are you?" Lucia asked.

"Nineteen."

"Yeah? I figured you for 17 or so. You aren't running away from your folks or anything, are you?"

"No—my folks are dead."

Lucia lowered her eyes. "I'm sorry, kid," she said. "I didn't mean to run you through the wringer. Look, what kind of work are you looking for?"

Rita shrugged. "Something that will get me someplace, I guess. All the jobs in the *Times* either ask for more experience than I have or don't lead anywhere."

"I know what you mean. You know, you've got a damned pretty face. Those cheekbones and that mouth and all that glossy black hair—you might make it in a chorus line if you wanted to. Can you dance?"

"A little."

"Well, you don't have to be any prima ballerina for a revue or a floorshow. Sing?"

"Not too well. I can carry a tune."

"Hell, you're one up on me. How about your body? What do your legs look like?"

Rita colored.

"Look, don't turn green on me. Open your robe and let me have a look at you."

"I—I don't have anything on under my robe," Rita exclaimed. "I was getting ready to take a shower."

"So what? I've seen girls before. I see one every time I take a look in my mirror. Let's have a look at you."

Rita opened her robe and the blonde girl's eyes centered first on her breasts and then on her hips and legs.

"Stand up," Lucia ordered.

Rita stood up, shifting nervously from one foot to the other.

"Now take the damned robe off and toss it on the bed."

Rita did as she was told. Lucia walked toward her, an empty glass in one hand and her eyes fixed on Rita's body. She put one hand on Rita's shoulder, squeezing the firm flesh slightly for a moment and then letting her fingers trail gently down Rita's bare arm.

"God," she said. "You really are beautiful, kiddo. You wouldn't even have to dance much with a shape like that."

"You think I could really get a job?"

"If you want to. Hell, it can be a lousy racket. You sit and wait for a break and eat every meal out of cans. You walk out of the theatre and every crumb within spitting distance thinks you're fair game for a roll in the hay. But you always think about the big break—it's a living, if you aren't too crazy about eating."

Rita hardly heard what Lucia was saying. In her mind she could already see her name in lights, could already hear the applause at the end of the show. It didn't seem possible—all she had ever done was a little singing and acting in high school plays. But Lucia seemed to know what she was talking about.

Lucia took a step back, her eyes still carefully appraising Rita's body. Somehow the blonde girl's eyes seemed to burn into Rita's flesh and she felt herself beginning to blush. It was silly, she thought angrily. It was just another girl looking at her, the same as the times she had undressed in the same room with one of her sisters, or the times when she and Lola would examine each other to see whose breasts had grown the most, or . . .

But there was something in the way Lucia stared at her that was different.

"You can get a job," Lucia was saying. "I got an agent, one of the best in the business. Believe me, he has to be good to get work for me. All I got is two legs and two of these" —she put her hands to her breasts— "and that's not enough to get a gal anyplace special. But Anthony Danton knows what strings to pull."

"Is that his name?"

"That's it, and he's big and tough and hungry for a buck. I'll give you his card—he's just a few blocks from here and you can run over to his office tomorrow morning. Tell him I sent you— that'll at least get you past the receptionist if nothing else. From there on in you're on your own."

"But what will I tell him?"

"Tell him you want a job. You do, don't you?"

"Yes, but—"

"No buts. You tell him you want a job and a good look at the way you're put together ought to swing it. Danton's got eyes, honey. And you're good to look at."

Rita felt herself blushing again.

"Don't be embarrassed. Look, in a business like this the way you look is half of your future. You'll have to get used to trying your damnedest to look beautiful and having men stare at you. You know what a chorus line is?"

"Of course."

"Know what it's there for?"

Rita looked blank.

"It's so a bunch of hard-up bastards can have something nice to look at. You get on the stage and shake your tail a little and every clod in the audience gets a real boost out of giving you the eye. Then each clod goes home to his wife and has a better time in bed because he got all hot and bothered looking at you."

"But—"

Lucia shook her head. "Honey, that's all there is to it. Wherever you are in this business it's 90% sex. You can be the best actress or dancer in creation, but if you don't make a man want to rip your clothes off and haul you down on the floor you have a hell of a hard time getting anywhere. And you said you wanted to get someplace, didn't you?"

"More than I want anything else."

"So what are you worrying about? Look, a chorus line doesn't have to be the last stop on the line. It will be for me; I haven't got enough talent to thread a needle with. Me, I got a guy lined up, a guy with enough money to thread all the needles in the world. I'm going to marry the slob and get out of this business after a while. But you might have the stuff. Who knows?"

Rita nodded slowly. Things were moving quickly and she wanted to be alone for awhile, alone so that she could digest all the new patterns Lucia had introduced and figure out just where she was. It seemed ages since she had left her mother, ages since Pardo had taken her in his arms. And yet it was less than a day since she had left Miami.

Lucia seemed to sense that she wanted time to think. "I don't want to crowd you," she said. "Tony's office is at 65 West 44th Street. Write it down."

Rita slipped her robe on again, took a pencil from her dresser drawer and jotted down the address on a slip of paper.

"You just tell him I sent you," Lucia said. "And tell me how you make out. Now I'll give you a chance to grab a shower and put in some time in the sack."

She retrieved her bottle and glasses and walked to the door. "You're okay, Rita Martin," she said. "I think we'll get along fine." She winked, and then she was gone.

Rita lay down on the bed again, her mind filled with pictures of dancers on a stage and actresses and actors batting lines back and forth. She thought about Lucia Fallon—the girl was unlike anybody she had ever met, and yet she was so friendly, so easy to talk to. She thought for a moment of Pardo, wishing she was with him and at the same time glad to be by herself.

New York was exciting. Even without leaving her little room New York had become exciting, and she was no longer worried about having nothing to do and no place to go. There would be plenty of everything for her—she was sure of it.

The shower was hot and the cold shower afterwards tingled and stimulated her skin. She toweled herself dry and slipped between the sheets of her bed, sleeping naked as she always did. Images floated through her mind and a smile came to her lips as she realized that everybody in New York was happily unaware that she was a little Cuban girl named Rita Morales whose mother was a whore and who had a month to go before her sixteenth birthday.

She smiled again.

And then she was asleep.

Chapter 4

Anthony Danton made a thick oak desk look like a matchbox. The man didn't sit, Rita thought. He loomed. He filled up his chair with his huge body and filled the office with cigar smoke while he listened to her, his face never changing expression.

The cigar remained all the while in the corner of his mouth, clamped between two rows of large white teeth. His shirt sleeves were rolled up and the muscles were visible in his forearms. He wasn't wearing a tie; the top button of his white shirt was open and Rita could see the thick hair on his chest.

She started by telling him Lucia had recommended him and finished by telling him that she wanted a job. In the middle came a list of her "credits"—work she had done before. The list was a lie, but she hoped that he wouldn't bother to check up on her. She had given him the names of a half-dozen clubs in Miami where she claimed to have worked in a chorus line, but the clubs were second and third-rate tourist traps and he might believe her easily enough.

She finished, and Anthony Danton's face still didn't change. She wondered what he was thinking, wondered what was going through the mind behind the steel-blue eyes.

Danton took the cigar from his mouth and flicked the ashes at an ashtray which nestled in the middle of a pile of papers on his desk. He missed the ashtray.

"You want a job," he said. It was neither a statement nor a question but somewhere in between.

Rita nodded.

"Chorus work."

She hesitated, then nodded again.

"Strip."

At first she thought she hadn't heard him correctly. Then she blushed. Danton noticed her blush, closing his eyes and shaking his head.

"Get outta here," he said. "Fast."

"But—"

The eyes snapped open suddenly. "Get outta here. You never worked in a club. You never worked anywhere, except maybe some charity show or high school bit. What are you wasting my time for?"

Her face fell. "How did you know?"

"Because you're afraid to drop your goddam pants, that's how. You worked in those strip joints on the Beach and you'da been out of your clothes half a minute after you walked into this office. You wouldn't even bother to shut the door if you knew what was coming off."

"Why?"

"Huh?" His eyebrows went up a notch and he bit harder on the cigar. "Because that's all a chorus girl is," he said. "A chorus girl can have two left legs as long as they're good legs. A chorus girl can have a voice for calling hogs if she looks good enough. All a chorus girl is, is a whore who doesn't put out, and all the customer's buying is her body to look at. And any chorus babe who thinks anybody's gonna waste time with her while she keeps her clothes on is nuts.

"So get out. And tell Lucia any time she sends over a school-girl again she can find herself another agent. I don't have to waste my time on her. I got a whole stable full of broads who can give her cards and spades and—"

"Shut up."

Danton's eyes widened and he almost bit the cigar in two. Rita knew she had made a mistake, but it had only taken her a minute to realize that she had to correct it. Her hands flew to the top of her blouse and she pulled it apart, not wasting time with the buttons. The buttons popped and the blouse opened.

She unhooked her black skirt and stepped out of it, kicking her shoes off at the same time. She removed the blouse and dropped it to the floor, her eyes never leaving Danton's face, her whole body upright and proud.

"I told you to shut up," she said. "Now you can tell me whether you can sell this body to a chorus line."

He was silent but his eyes were busy. Surprisingly, Rita didn't blush under his gaze. There was something completely impersonal about the way he was looking at her, as if she were a slab of meat in a butcher shop. He was appraising her body professionally, and any sexual hunger was absent from his eyes.

"Turn around," he said.

Rita turned around. She wondered for a moment whether anyone in the outer office could see her through the translucent window in the office door, deciding quickly that it didn't matter in the least.

Danton's words had kindled a spark in her. She was going to make the grade, going to make more money and meet more people and get further than a hell of a lot of other girls, and if that meant somebody had to stare at her body she couldn't care less. She could feel herself toughening up inside and she was more conscious of the determination growing inside of her than she was of Danton's eyes on her bare body.

"Turn around again."

She followed his instructions. "I could take my panties off too," she suggested. "Just in case you want a better look at me."

For the first time the shadow of a smile crossed the agent's face. "Leave 'em on," he said. "They're thin enough so's they don't hide much."

She didn't blush.

"You got guts," he said. "You haven't got a hell of a lot in the brain department, but you don't need a head if you got the kind of body you got. But how much do you have in the way of experience? And cut the crapola this time."

She told him the truth, mentioning the few shows at the high school in Miami.

"And how old are you? And no bull."

"Nineteen."

He considered for a moment. "Look," he said, "I might place you. You look good enough, that's for sure. But it's almost impossible to land a show biz job for a Spic in this town. Why don't you get into something else?"

"I'm not a—"

"The hell you're not," he cut in. "Look, I couldn't care less if you're a goddam Chinaman, see? But the guys who do the book-ing don't figure that way nine times out of ten. And—"

"I'm not a Spic," she said. The word wasn't one she had used before, but that didn't stop her. Nothing was going to stop her.

"Everybody takes me for a lousy Spic," she went on. "I'm damned sick of it."

"Yeah? What's your real name?"

"The one I gave you. Rita Martin."

"Sure. Sure, that's why you look like a Spic—because your name's Martin. Your folks come over on the *Mayflower*?"

She hesitated—then she had an inspiration. "It used to be Martino," she said. "I changed it."

"Martino?"

"That's right. I'm Italian."

The big man broke into laughter, and he laughed the way only a big man can laugh. It seemed to Rita as though the walls were going to come down.

"I'll be damned," he said. "I'll be a son of a bitch. Martino, meet a *paisan*."

She looked blank.

"Tonio D'Annunzio," he said. "Alias Anthony Danton. You silly little broad, why the hell didn't you tell me your real moni-ker right away? Didn't Lucia tell you I'm nothing but another guinea?"

"No," she said. "I—"

He laughed again. "Put your clothes on," he said. "And here's a couple safety pins for that blouse—that act you put on was cute, but it raised hell with the buttons."

•   •   •

While she dressed, Danton told her what she would have to do if she was going to make the grade. "You'll make lousy money," he told her. "A yard a week tops, and ten percent of that goes to me—leaving you ninety. You'll work long hours and guys'll ask you to go to bed with 'em now and then—but whether you do or not is up to you.

"As far as getting anywhere, that depends on what kind of breaks you get. A press agent would help, but most of them are crooks and the rest want too much of your dough.

"I like you, Rita. I'll do what I can for you. But from now on you better level with me. Understand?"

"I understand." She fastened the safety pins to hold her blouse together and pulled her skirt into place.

"You got a good build," he said. "Good legs, good chest, and a cute rear. Your face is good too, and that's not so common in this business. You might make it."

"I'm going to make it."

He shrugged. "All of you are. Every gal who walks in that door thinks she'll wind up in Hollywood, but most of 'em wind up having babies and washing diapers. Or walking the streets."

"That won't happen to me."

He shrugged again. "Maybe yes, maybe no. Long as I get my ten percent it don't matter too much. You still want a job?"

"Of course."

"I got a call that there's an opening at the Cinderella. You know the club?"

"No."

"Strip joint down in the Village on Third Street. Couple blocks east of Sixth. It's a trap—the drinks are cut with shellac and the food is poison. But nobody goes there to eat. They go there to stare at the broads.

"There's a headliner, a specialty act and a chorus. You can work into the chorus if you make it. The manager's a guy name of Finch, a tight little bastard with a face like a hungry rat and a mind like a sewer. He'll probably try to lay you."

"I can handle him."

He shrugged again. "I don't care whether you lay for him or not," he said. "That's between the two of you. Just don't ball it up so you don't get the job. Okay?"

"Okay."

"This week the headliner's a gal name of Flame. She does this bit with a fire—there's a kind of chemical that burns at a low temperature and she rubs this fire all over her body and sort of wiggles around. She doesn't get hot but the customers do. Get it?"

She nodded.

"The specialty act's an acrobat named Annie Cross. She's kind of skinny but her boobs are fairly big—I think she gives herself paraffin injections so's they stay firm. She does this contortionist routine that winds up giving guys brand new ideas of how to make love to their wives. If they try it they'll pull a muscle in their back, but the hell with them. You get the picture?"

She nodded again.

"There may be a comic. Comics I don't handle, because comics I can't stand, but there may be a comic. All you gotta worry about is looking sexy. Think you can look sexy?"

"Yes."

"Yeah, you can. You go down and see Finch about six or seven tonight. I'll give him a buzz and tell him you're coming down. And you're name's Martin, Rita Martin, and for chrissake's tell him you're 21. You got any identification says you're 21?"

"No."

"I'll fix it for you. Gimme your address and phone on a sheet of paper and I'll get a guy to make out a driver's license for you. You registered at your room as Martin?"

"Yes."

"Then that's your name. No more Martino, and if you got friends in New York you can tell 'em your name's Martin from now on. Got it?"

She nodded again.

"Get outta here," he said again, but the edge to this voice was friendly this time. "You gotta have a cabaret card to work in a club in this town, but I'll get that taken care of. That'll come out of your first week's pay along with my cut. Finch'll tell you he'll give you eighty, but you tell him a hundred or it's off. You'll get the hundred."

"Are you sure he'll hire me?"

"Get outta here," Danton snapped. "He'll hire you. Now leave me alone."

Rita didn't realize how lucky she was until she told Lucia what had happened. Then she learned that nightclub work was highly prized, and that a good many girls in the business prized it above musicals and revues. A Broadway show could fold on you the day after it opened, but a stint at a club could—and often did—last almost forever. Lucia was working at The Play Pen, a strip club on 52nd Street. Years ago, just after the war, 52nd Street had been dotted with jazz clubs at the time when progressive jazz was just beginning to emerge. Now the jazz clubs had changed to strip joints, and Lucia's private name for the place she worked was The Pig Pen.

Burlesque was illegal in New York, but Rita learned that the law only served to eliminate the old-style burlesque house and substitute the cheap nightclub for it. Strippers were billed as *exotic dancers* and the business went on in the same old way, while the die-hard burlesque fans went across the river to Newark or Union City if they rebelled at the idea of paying a dollar and a half for a shot of watered-down rye.

When Rita got to the Cinderella, a quick glance showed that the place was hardly the last word in class. It was cheap and gaudy, with the owner cutting corners in expenses by providing cheap flashy uniforms for the waitresses and cigarette girls and similarly keeping the cost down for the furniture and lighting fixtures.

The ancient Negro who was sweeping the floor very methodically directed Rita to Jacob Finch's office, his eyes only stopping for a moment to study the breasts that strained against the girl's black sweater. Walking to Finch's office, Rita wondered whether she had chosen the right clothes for the interview. A dress might have made her look older, but the black sweater and tight green skirt showed off her shape better than any of the dresses she and Pardo had picked out.

Finch's office door was open, and the picture of the little man behind the desk contrasted so dramatically with the memory of Anthony Danton behind a similar desk that Rita almost laughed.

The desks were identical—massive oak affairs piled high with papers and publicity photos. But the men were as different as day and night.

Jacob Finch did not look exactly like a hungry rat. He looked more like a rabid weasel. His eyes were beady and black and protruded from a thin, pimply face. His chin came to a sharp point, and his brown hair was piled back on his head like a heap of dung-colored straw. He was far and away the most unattractive man Rita could remember ever seeing, but that wasn't all there was to it.

He looked mean, mean and sniveling and sneaky. He looked as though he would gleefully cut out a man's heart for a dollar and then try to sell the heart to a dissecting laboratory. His mouth was closed and he was too far away for her to smell him, but Rita was willing to bet that his teeth were discolored and his breath stank. He was that type of man.

He looked up and smiled. "You're the gal Danton sent over," he said. "What's your name again?"

She told him.

"Not bad," he said, looking her over carefully. She shifted uncomfortably under his gaze, feeling as though she was being undressed and caressed with dirty hands.

"Can you dance?"

She nodded.

"Sing?"

"Yes."

He pointed to her breasts. "Those all yours?"

"Yes."

"Let's see them."

She pulled the sweater over her head, noting how different Finch's reaction was from that of her agent. He looked at her breasts as if he wanted to devour them one at a time and he made her feel dirty, dirty and cheap.

"No bra," he said. "Not bad." He pulled a cigarette from a half-crumpled pack and stuck it between his lips. Then he lit the cigarette with a match and extinguished the match with a puff of smoke.

"Strip down," he said. "I want a look at your legs, too."

She wanted to strip as quickly as possible, to get it over with in a rush so that she could get away from him and back to her room. He made her sick to her stomach, this little man with beady eyes and a pimply face.

But she knew that she had to make him want her if she wanted the job, and at the moment the job was the most important thing in the world to her. And so she stripped slowly, very slowly and almost languorously, letting her fingers play with the button on the skirt and toy with the zipper, opening the skirt and pulling it down ever so gently over her full hips and swelling thighs.

His eyes fastened on her panties and she knew that he was trying to see straight through them, trying to imagine what it would be like to be in bed with her, what her body would be like pressing and straining against his. The thought of it nauseated her, but she forced herself to make him want her.

She didn't remove her shoes. She was wearing black pumps with high spike heels, and she knew that they made her legs look even better. After a few moments she stood before him, naked except for the panties and the shoes.

It was warm in the office. The presence of Jacob Finch made it seem unbearably hot.

He leaned over and stabbed out his cigarette in an ashtray. Then he stood up and stepped out from behind the desk, walking toward her slowly. She didn't move, hoping he would stay away from her and at the same time he would desire to come closer.

He came closer. He kept coming closer until he was inches away from her, and as he walked she couldn't mistake the pure animal hunger in his eyes as they roamed over her body.

Then he touched her. His hand was thin and bony and there was dirt under his nails, and his hand rested on her shoulder and kneaded me flesh gently. She wanted to cringe, to be sick.

But she didn't dare.

His hand moved, tracing a course from her shoulder to her breast. His fingers brushed her breast gently and cupped it, and she knew that she would have to bathe herself over and over before she would feel clean again.

He squeezed her breast, then relaxed his fingers. He squeezed her again, harder this time, and it hurt her.

She thought of this man making love to her, getting in bed with her and . . .

She prayed that he would be satisfied with less than that.

He stepped still closer to her without letting go of her breast and his other arm encircled her back. His fingers found the elastic band on her panties and pulled at it.

Blue panties, she thought. *Because it's Monday*. And she thought of Pardo and remembered how different it had been when he touched her, how the feelings that went through her then were so different from the ones going through her right now.

He pressed her to him, his body hard and insistent against hers. He slipped his hand inside her panties and touched her, stroking her. She wanted to cry out—but she couldn't.

He tugged again at her panties and they fell to the floor. He kissed her clumsily, his breath as foul as she expected, and then released her momentarily to fumble with his own clothing.

Then he was holding her again, whispering filthy words into her ear and pinching and hurting her tender flesh. He pushed her down onto the floor and the rug was rough and harsh under her skin.

Then he took her, and even as she feigned passion and went through the motions of love her stomach seemed prepared to turn over. She thought that the job couldn't be worth it, that nothing could be worth this, and she wanted only to be away from him, away by herself with no one around her, no one to bother her, no hands to touch her and no mouth to seek hers.

His fingers found the nipple of her right breast, and at the critical moment he squeezed her as hard as he possibly could. She let out an agonized moan.

And then it was over.

CHAPTER 5

"No more," she told him. "Never again. That was to get the job, but it won't happen again."

He nodded, agreeing. He hadn't told her that she was hired and she hadn't asked; this was something to be taken for granted. Now that the act was completed and the job hers she suddenly felt much older. It was as much of a step for her as it had been to lose her virginity to Pardo.

She felt not like a whore but like a businesswoman. She hadn't sold anything; she had exchanged her body for a chance, and she knew that it was an exchange she would be willing to make in the future. With Pardo she had started as a whore and wound up as a woman. With Finch she had remained on the same level from beginning to end.

The business level. The exchange, straight and simple and that was all there was to it.

She started that night. There was a brief rehearsal where one of the five other girls, a tall brunette named Sharon, taught her the steps she would go through in the course of the dance routine.

It was a simple dance. All she had to do, really, was to show the men what sort of body she had. The girls didn't strip in the general sense of the word. In their first number they came on the stage wearing white skirts and abbreviated black blouses. Midway through the number the skirts went and they finished in the blouses and white panties.

The other number followed the same pattern, with blue skirts giving way to blue panties and an orange western-style blouse giving way to an orange halter. The dances themselves were so easy that Rita knew the job would be no trouble at all, and she was pleased to notice that she was at least as good a dancer as Sharon. She was also a good deal better looking than Sharon, for that matter, and that made her feel even better.

The first show started at ten, and she killed two hours eating a leisurely dinner in a Village restaurant and wandering around the area. The meal was good—chicken tetrazzini with red wine in a small Italian restaurant. *Eating Italian food*, she thought. *Sure, and my name's really Rita Martino and I'm Italian*. She smiled to herself, remembering the conversation with Danton.

After dinner, walking around the area, she decided that she liked Greenwich Village. It was less harsh and foreboding than the rest of New York. The buildings were not so tall, for one thing, and the funny little shops and the men with beards and girls with no lipstick and thick eye makeup seemed interesting.

She thought that it might be good to live here, near her job and away from all the hustle and turmoil of midtown Manhattan. Maybe she and Lucia could share an apartment. That would be good—they could cook dinners themselves and save as much money as they were saving now by living in furnished rooms.

Besides, there was something wrong about having a single room all by herself. It was only her second day in New York, but already she could see that she would be lonely in a room all alone, with four walls and a ceiling to keep her company and no way to break the monotony.

She wandered around, studying the people who were somehow different from the average New Yorkers, noting the coffee houses and the strip clubs looking incongruous next to one another.

By the time the show went on she was kindled to a fever pitch. The interview with Danton, the hellish hour with Finch, the meal and the walk—everything was happening with incredible speed and she could hardly keep up with it. She got into costume quickly, running through the routine swiftly with Sharon and then ready to go on.

The show started. The MC was a man named Lucky White, a 40-ish, balding comic on the way down who introduced the acts and doubled in brass as a comedian between the feature and the second chorus number. He laid down a line of third-rate patter and wound up by saying that the Cinderella girls were coming on now and everybody should give them a big hand.

Everybody did, but everybody on a Monday night at ten o'clock meant about a dozen people. A piano, bass and drums made quiet music and the number started.

The dance number didn't seem to take any time at all. Surprisingly, Rita wasn't the least bit nervous. It seemed perfectly natural to dance around on a postage-stamp stage with a spotlight on her tanned skin, and if she had ever had any qualms about letting men look at her, the tussle with her boss had ended that for good.

At the same time, she discovered that the glamour she was looking for was also missing. Making good in the world seemed to be more a case of pushing ahead than one of getting happier and happier. She had to admit to herself that the only exciting thing about performing at the Cinderella was the money and a chance for something bigger.

The Cinderella itself was as dull as dishwater.

After her own act had finished, Rita had a chance to watch the rest of the show from off-stage. Annie Cross, the contortionist, was different from anything she had ever seen before. The slender girl seemed to be made out of elastic, twisting into impossible positions in time to an erotic drum beat.

She stood with her feet planted on the stage and bent back slowly, rolling her hips all the while in a sensuous rhythm. She kept bending in what seemed to be an impossible manner until her head touched the floor and her high breasts pointed at the ceiling. She was wearing a black leotard that left her arms and legs bare and covered her from her neck to her thighs, and the second her head touched the floor she pulled a string and the leotard fell away.

Rita could hear every man in the crowd catch his breath. Annie Cross appeared to be nude, with a flesh-colored G-string and two gold sequins the only protection her body enjoyed. And, despite what Danton had said, Annie Cross had an extremely passable body.

Then the girl began to writhe spasmodically, her whole body twisting. Her breasts shook with the motion and her hips threw out an unmistakable message.

Annie raised herself slightly on her hands and moved her head forward, bringing it slowly forward until she was bent double and her face looked out at the audience from between her legs.

She smiled. Then she wiggled and smiled again.

And the audience loved it.

But it was Flame who revealed to Rita what a sexual dance really was. Annie, she could see readily enough, was exciting largely because she was different, a talented freak. She supplied her audience with new ideas, new possibilities, and that was what made them want to watch her.

Flame was different.

Flame had red hair, the perfect sort of red hair that goes with a milk-white complexion, deep and burnished red hair. Rita knew from a close look at the start that Flame's beautiful red hair came out of a bottle, but the men in the audience had no way of telling this.

Flame's skin hadn't come out of a bottle, and it was as exciting as her hair. There was not a blemish on her creamy thighs or her graceful, slender neck. Her breasts were unbelievably large without being gross or flabby in the least.

Flame was a big woman—close to six feet tall, with wide hips and full breasts and rounded, well-muscled legs. And Flame had an act that was as unique as Annie's without being freakish in the least.

Rita watched the star with her eyes wide. She sat by herself on the sidelines, not talking to anyone and noticing nothing but the girl who occupied the spotlight. The music was very soft now, but there was an unmistakable drive to it—a drive matched by Flame's insistent motion and the noticeable hunger that surged through the audience.

Flame was not a stripper. She didn't shed a bit of clothing on stage, walking onstage in a black bra and G-string and walking offstage exactly the same.

She didn't have to undress.

The curtain went up with a pot of fire blazing in the center of the stage. Then Flame walked out, her eyes on the fire and her body moving sensuously. She walked to the pot of fire and writhed in front of it, as if it were very hot but she could resist it no more than a moth could resist a flame.

She dipped one hand through the fire, then the other. She repeated the process several times, each time letting her hands remain a trifle longer in the flame.

Then she scooped up a handful of the burning chemicals and rubbed them against her bare belly.

She danced, writhing and twisting as if the fire were burning her. She dipped again and again into the pot of burning chemicals, rubbing the fire all over her body until she appeared to be a human torch. The fire stood out on her breasts and she rolled back and forth dizzily, her proud breasts flaming and rolling from side to side. She dipped over once again and pressed a handful of fire between her legs, dipping and bending and shrieking in mock agony.

Then the lights went out. Nothing could be seen but the fire burning on her body as she moved back and forth in an orgy of primitive lust. The lights came on, slowly, very slowly.

The tempo increased. The music increased in pitch. Flame danced faster, faster. She whirled in a little circle, burning furiously.

Then she shrieked once and the curtain fell.

•   •   •

Lucia nodded when Rita told her about Flame's act. "I worked with her once," she said. "Flame never plays a club long; none of the top girls do. She gets around $500 a week and runs the whole circuit. Travels across the whole damned country."

"$500 a week?"

"Maybe more. Isn't that one hell of an act she's got?"

Rita nodded. "How can she keep from getting burned?"

"It's a chemical fire. You ever fill a cigarette lighter and spill liquid on your hand?"

"I don't smoke."

"I forgot. Well, if you do and then flick the lighter before the fluid evaporates, sometimes your whole hand'll be burning without hurting at all. The fluid burns at a low temperature and doesn't get hot enough to hurt you."

"I see."

"And with Flame," Lucia went on, "it's something that burns at a lower temperature than lighter fluid. I don't know what the hell she uses but it sure works all right."

Rita nodded. She stretched out on her bed while Lucia went on talking to her, but somehow she couldn't keep her mind on what the girl was saying. She was too mixed up.

She was earning $100 a week; $90 after Anthony Danton had his share. She was living 1500 miles away from home with a new name, and she was working at a nightclub, and that afternoon a man had made love to her on the floor of his office.

And three days ago—

She didn't think about three days ago, pushing it forcibly from her mind. She couldn't afford to think back. Things were going to happen quickly; as soon as they stopped happening quickly she would be standing still, and as soon as that happened she might as well stop living.

She was earning $100 a week, which was more money than she could have imagined when home was a dump on Flagler Street. But Flame was earning $500 a week, and somewhere there were other girls with a good deal more money than that.

She opened her eyes, still not listening to Lucia. The memory of Jake Finch stuck in her mind and she couldn't dislodge it. Why did she have to go through something like that to get places? She knew that she would never let Finch have her again, but she knew that there would be other men like Finch. While she couldn't believe anybody would be quite so bad, there would be others, and she was smart enough to know that it took more than money to wind up on Golden Beach.

A woman had to be respectable as well. And respectability didn't mix with round heels.

It was a problem. Long after Lucia left she lay motionless on the bed, trying to figure out where she was going. Even Flame had not reached the goal Rita had set for herself, and Flame was making at least five times as much money. Flame never would reach that goal. Flame would always be a nightclub dancer, and that would mean that the world would always think of her as a high-priced whore.

Was that what the men in the audience thought of Rita? She wondered for a moment; then she decided that they probably hadn't noticed her at all. If they did, by now she wasn't even a memory.

But people were going to notice her.

She closed her eyes and slipped further under the covers. She let her hands run easily over her body, glad that the shower had been able to wash the stench of Jake Finch from her skin.

It was a good body, she decided. She smiled lazily, remembering that four persons had appraised that body in the last three days. First there was Pardo, then Lucia, then Danton and finally Finch.

And then, of course, there had been a whole roomful of customers at the Cinderella.

It was a good body. A good many people were going to admire that body in the next few months, but she decided that she wasn't going to try to parlay her body into a fortune via the strip clubs. There had to be a better way, a way that would let her be rich and respectable, a way that would lead to Golden Beach without turning her into a high-class hustler.

My mother is a whore, she thought suddenly. She knew that she was still the daughter of Carmen Morales, and that all the breaks in the world would not alter that one simple fact. Her mother was a whore, a woman who gave herself to men for money.

She had to be very careful.

Again she ran her hands over her body. Perhaps there would be a man who would want that body in a way that was different from Jacob Finch and Luis Pardo. Perhaps she could meet a rich man, a man who would want her to marry him.

Would a man be ashamed to marry a chorus girl? Not necessarily, she decided. If she kept herself good, if she was not too easy for a man to coax into bed, then some man might want her to marry him. She realized suddenly that the easiest way to wind up on Golden Beach was to marry someone who already lived there.

Much easier than trying to lay her way to the top. Much easier than saving up her pennies and trying to turn herself into the hottest stripper in show business.

A rich man, she thought. Not too old and not too young, and it was not absolutely necessary that he be the richest man in the world. A good man, an honest man, a man she could look up to with respect and a man who could tell her she was the most wonderful woman in the world.

She remembered the man in the Corvette, the man in the white dinner jacket whom she had seen from the schoolhouse window.

A man like that, she thought.

Could a man like that take her? She was lovely enough, and she was certainly intelligent enough, and she could surely make such a man a good wife.

Would he mind that she was a chorus girl?

No, she decided. No, the son of man she wanted would not mind something like that.

But would he mind that her mother was a Cuban prostitute living in a one-room shack on the Flagler Street docks?

That he would mind. And that, she decided firmly, he would never know.

CHAPTER 6

The letter came three days later.

She hadn't expected a letter. She never bothered looking for mail, never even thought about it. She had buried herself in a small world inhabited only by Lucia, Danton, the people at the Cinderella. And by herself.

Mostly by herself, because although she talked to Lucia daily there was little deep feeling between them. And she hadn't seen Danton at all, nor had she exchanged more than three sentences at a time with any of the others. She lived alone by herself in her own little world.

Until the letter came.

She found the letter under her door one night when she came home from work. It was addressed to *Rita Martin* and she thought that it must be from Danton or the club. Then she saw the Miami postmark and she was lost, because nobody at all in Miami knew where she was living.

And nobody at all in Miami knew that her name was now Rita Martin.

She kicked off her shoes absently and sat down on the bed, holding the letter in her right hand and staring at it without seeing it. She was tired; it had been a hard night at the club. She was tired, and she had come home expecting to take a fast shower and go to sleep right away. And here was this letter.

She ripped open the envelope and took out the single sheet of paper. She unfolded the paper and read the letter from beginning to end. Then she read it a second time, slowly.

The letter said:

> Rita:
>
> I found out where you were living from a friend. No matter how many times you move I will find out where you are. I also found out your name.
>
> I want you back. I love you and I need you and you do not belong in New York. You belong here with me. I can give you everything you need and more.
>
> Write to me. I will send you plane fare and you can come back to me and be with me.
>
> If you wish it we will be married.
>
> > Pardo

She read the letter a third time with her face absolutely expressionless. Then she stood up, still holding the letter in her hand, and she walked back and forth across the floor of the little room. She paced the floor several times, still holding onto the letter, still without any trace of expression in her eyes. Then she tore the letter in half and in half again and dropped the pieces into the wastebasket.

•   •   •

When she opened her eyes the next morning Lucia was sitting on the edge of her bed smiling down at her. She was wearing her bathrobe—a white, terry-cloth affair that could be a bathrobe and still show off her full-blown figure to great advantage. Her eyes were wide awake and the lipstick was fresh on her generous mouth.

"Hi," she said. "Christ, it's past two already. What time did you get to bed?"

"I don't know. About five, I guess. Why?"

"No reason. I've been waiting for you to get up for an hour at least. You know, you've got the dullest damned room in the world."

Rita sat up and looked around, raising the bedsheet to cover her breasts as she did so. "What do you mean?"

"I mean it's dull. God, you don't have a picture on the wall or a scatter rug on the floor or anything. How do you stand it?"

"I don't mind."

"I would. I think I'd go out of my mind in a day staring at four blank walls. They're not even good-looking walls, either."

"I don't mind them. I mean, it's just a place to sleep."

Lucia nodded. "That's just what I mean. It should be more than just a place to sleep. You've been here less than a week, but wait until you've been around for a month or two. It'll drive you batty."

"Isn't your room the same?"

Lucia shook her head. "It was. I bought some prints over on Sixth Avenue and plastered them all over the walls. And some dirty pictures."

"What?"

"Dirty pictures."

"I—"

"They're a kick. You know, pornography. Want to have a look?"

Rita was uncertain. She still couldn't figure the older girl out. She seemed so strange, so totally different from anyone she had known before. It was obvious that she was a friend, the way she helped her find a job and all. But she still couldn't quite figure Lucia out.

"C'mon," Lucia said. "Get out of that bed and get dressed."

For emphasis she grasped Rita's hand and gave her a tug from the bed. Rita dressed in a hurry, slipping on a white blouse and a pair of checkered slacks, and the two went across the little hallway to Lucia's room.

Rita noticed the prints first—they were larger than the photographs and more colorful. There was a Matisse print of a girl looking into her mirror and several impressionist prints which Rita half-recognized from the art classes she took in high school but couldn't identify.

Then she noticed the pictures.

There were over twenty of them, and they were spread out equally over the four walls of Lucia's room. Rita stared at them with a sort of morbid fascination, wanting to leave and at the same time wanting to see more. They were the same type of pictures one of the seniors had sold in her high school in Miami, but they were far worse.

Or better, she decided. Depending how you looked at it.

There were pictures of men and women and of women and women. There were pictures of the sex act in every position Rita had ever known of and several she hadn't believed possible. There was a picture of two women engaged in an act that made her sick to her stomach, and one large picture of two men and two women in a sickeningly and strangely exciting orgiastic display.

She stared at them in silence, one at a time. No detail escaped her notice. She saw the expressions on the faces of the men and women, saw the beads of sweat on their bodies and the way their muscles contracted.

Then, on the far wall, she saw pictures that made the others look tame. There was a picture of a man and a small boy, and one of a gigantic man and two tiny girls. There was a picture of a man, naked, lashing a women's bare back with his whip.

And there were others, each one different from the last.

"Well?" Lucia asked expectantly. "How do you like my collection?"

"I—" Rita groped for the right word.

"You probably don't like them yet," Lucia said. "Most women don't. The guy who sold 'em to me was surprised—he said he hardly ever had a dame for a customer."

"Where did you get them?"

"Over on 42nd Street. You know all those bookstores?"

Rita nodded, remembering the little dingy bookstores that dotted the Times Square district.

Lucia chuckled. "They aren't bookstores," she said. "They are, but the books on their counters wouldn't pay the rent if they sold them by the carload. They make their money on these things," she added, pointing at the pictures.

"You mean they can just . . . sell things like that?"

"Not in the open. They keep them under the counter or in the back room. You go in and you tell the guy what you want and he gets it for you."

"Don't the police—"

"Not if the guys pay off. Hell, if you pay enough to the cops you can do just about anything in this town. Isn't it like that in Miami?"

Rita considered for a moment, remembering the way one of the men from the vice squad used to come to her mother twice a month for money. And she remembered the other one, the one who wanted something besides money.

"Yes," she said slowly. "I suppose it is. But why do you want . . . these?"

"They sparkle up a room. Look, you can't have a man up here so I have to settle for the next best thing. And it keeps the room from becoming too much of a bore. I can just sack out and stare at the pictures. You know, I've been thinking of buying some 8x10's and pasting them on the ceiling. Then I wouldn't have to crane my neck to look at them."

"But why do you like to look at them?"

Lucia stepped close to her, slipping her arm familiarly around Rita's waist. "Look at that one," she said, pointing to one of the pictures. "What do you feel when you look at it?"

Rita stared hard at the picture. It was a picture of two women in bed together, naked. She looked at them, looked at what they were doing to each other.

"How does it make you feel?"

"I . . . I don't know."

"Don't you get excited? Don't you want to know how it feels

to do what they're doing? Doesn't it make you sort of nervous inside?"

"I . . . it's just a picture," she continued lamely.

"Of course. It's just a picture, and you can watch it and get your kicks from it without getting hurt. You don't have to do anything. See?"

Rita nodded. She didn't quite understand what Lucia was getting at, but she let it drop. Her eyes flitted from one picture to the other against her will. She tried to direct her gaze to the floor, but each time her eyes returned to the pictures.

"What I really wanted to ask you," Lucia began, letting her arm drop from Rita's waist. "What I wanted to ask was if there's any guy in particular you're going with."

"No," Rita answered. "I haven't had a date since I came to New York."

"Want one?"

"Who with?"

"A hell of a nice guy. I've been dating a fellow named Phil Travis off and on for about three months. He's got this friend named Ned Barnes and Phil asked me if I could set up a date for Ned with some nice girl who was easy on the eyes. Naturally I thought of you."

"Thanks. But— What's Ned like?"

"Nice," Lucia said. "Fairly tall, blond hair cut short, light complexion, good talker—you'll like him."

"What does he do for a living?"

"Same as Phil—he runs copy at an ad agency on Madison Avenue."

"He's a copy boy?"

Lucia laughed. "Yes, but that doesn't mean he's some jerk stuck in a lousy job. He and Phil want to get some place in the advertising business, and in order to do that you have to start at the bottom. They're both 25 and they've been out of college for about four years now—two of them in the army. In a few months they'll be some kind of junior executive at the ad agency, and from there on they can scoot right up to the top if they're good enough."

"I see."

"So is it a date?"

"When? You didn't even tell me."

"Tonight."

"What time?"

Lucia thought for a moment. "Let's see," she said. "The Pig Pen closes at four, but I get off at three. How about you?"

"3:15."

"Swell—they can pick me up at three and then we'll come after you. Good enough?"

"Sure," Rita said. "What do I wear? Will we be going any place fancy?"

"You kidding? Not on the forty bucks a week these guys pull down. But I'll tell you, I'd rather stick along with a guy like Phil on his forty a week then try to play games with some playboy with a fat wallet. If I can hook Phil, he'll be making $15,000 in a few years—and I'll be living high off the hog in Connecticut."

"You want to marry him?"

Lucia nodded. "But forget I told you, huh? I want him to think he doped out the idea all by himself."

"Of course."

"And we'll pick you up when you get off from work."

Rita nodded, heading for the door. "Thanks for fixing me up," she said. "And for showing me your room."

"Think nothing of it," Lucia said. "You can come back any time you have a yen."

Back in her own room, Rita thought there was some extra meaning in Lucia's final words. But she couldn't tell exactly what it was.

The night was the same as the other nights at the Cinderella. Rita was beginning to realize that the nights at the Cinderella were always the same, with Lucky White telling the same off-color jokes and Annie Cross going through her same set of gyrations and Flame performing her ritual fire dance in the same manner as all the other nights. Rita and the other Cinderella girls went through their routines just as they did every night, and Rita knew that, since she had the steps and motions down pat, there would never be anything the least bit challenging about twisting around on the little stage.

It was, all things considered, a bore.

Next week things would change—a new headliner would replace Flame and a new name would appear in lights on the marquee. But everything else would remain basically the same.

She danced, going through the simple steps with no concern whatsoever for the eyes that followed her body. She finished the first show and changed her costume, waiting in the big dressing room while Annie Cross and Flame had their turns. Then the Cinderella girls took over and went through their second routine, and later they repeated the first routine once again as usual.

This was typical of a dump like the Cinderella, Rita had learned. Why bother with three sets of dances when nobody stayed for more than two shows?

But later, when she met Lucia and Phil Travis and Ned Barnes the night became a good deal more interesting. Ned himself was interesting, and she was pleased to discover that he was even more attractive than the picture Lucia had painted of him.

He was tall—over six feet tall, with his blond crewcut making him look like a kid in an Ivy League college. But the little lines at the corners of his mouth and the wrinkles beginning to form in his forehead destroyed the college kid image and created an interesting visual paradox.

He spoke with a slight twang to his voice, and when Rita found out he was from Iowa she was not surprised. He wasn't from a farm town, but from Des Moines—which he informed Rita was not a hick town at all but a rather pleasant place.

He told her he didn't want to go back to Des Moines, though. His father was a lawyer there with a fairly decent practice he could enter, but he preferred to leave the practice to his younger brother and strike out on his own. He wanted to make money in the ad game, he told her. He wanted a wife and kids and a house in Connecticut, so that he could be near New York and still have a big yard for his children to play in.

"Everybody wants to live in Connecticut," he said once. "All the boys in advertising want the same thing—a pleasant little rut where you race to catch the 8:02 in the morning and read the *Times* on the way to work and have two martinis at lunch and three when you get through and catch the 5:36 out of New York and read the *Telly* on the way home. It's supposed to be a rut, but I think I'll like it."

He tried to be casual about it, but Rita couldn't help seeing how enthusiastic and ambitious he was. She was pleased to see it, too, glad to find another person with the same fire she felt herself. Here was a guy who wanted to make it on his own and to make it big, and she was the kind of girl who wanted the same things. She liked him instantly.

The four of them went to a small Village bar around the corner from the Cinderella, and when the bar closed they went to the apartment on Bleecker Street that Phil and Ned were sharing. It was a nice apartment, cheaply but tastefully furnished and equipped with a well-stocked bar. They sat in a circle on the floor, talking constantly and drinking vodka and orange juice out of paper cups.

They drank heavily but the liquor didn't seem to affect anyone. The conversation was too intense for the liquor to gain hold of their minds or bodies. Rita learned a lot that night—about Ned, about Phil Travis, about Lucia and about life in general.

She learned the sort of life the two boys were leading—working very hard for very little money and praying for a break, a chance to step up from the mail clerk stage into copywriting, a chance to make a little more money each week and move up the ladder toward the top. She got an idea of the sort of circle they moved in, complete with girls trying to get a break in the acting world and guys from advertising and publishing and other talented people starting from the bottom.

None of them had much money. They couldn't go night-clubbing or to the theatre, so parties and drinks at cheap Village bars had to compensate for that type of a social life. They hung around in the Village because the informal atmosphere was a welcome change from the formality of their 9-to-5 routine, and they drank too much on the weekends and talked too much the rest of the time.

She decided that she liked them.

It was easy to let her mind wander even when the conversation was stimulating and exciting. It was easy to let her eyes focus on Ned's bright blue eyes and picture that home in Connecticut he talked about, easy to think of herself as sharing that home with him. The would be perfect, she decided. That would be the top, or as close to the top as she would have to go.

Ned Barnes. Rita Barnes, nee Rita Martin, nee Rita Martino, nee Rita Morales. She pictured herself cooking breakfast for Ned, kissing him goodbye when he went to meet his train and kissing him hello when she picked him up at the station in the evening. She imagined him rising in the advertising world and imagined herself rising with him, growing as her man grew and sharing a life with him.

Of course it was ridiculous, she told herself. She hardly knew him, and she certainly couldn't imagine herself to be in love with him, not after knowing him for a scant three hours. But sitting in the apartment and watching the sky lighten through the window as the morning came over New York, she felt certain that he liked her and that she would see him again.

Phil Travis, she decided, was a different matter. In a way he was a good deal more exciting than Ned, with his hair as black as her own and his eyebrows thick and bushy. He was short and wiry, his eyes constantly darting around the room and his conversation always quick, always sharp and provocative. But while she knew instinctively that Ned was a man who could be trusted, she knew just as surely that she could never trust Phil Travis with anything. He was that sort of a man. She wondered idly whether Lucia was sleeping with him or not. The way he looked at her, with a sort of possessive look in his brown eyes, made her suspect that this was the case. But she had a vague notion that Lucia wouldn't sleep with him—not until she managed to get a diamond ring on her finger. Not for any moral reasons, because Rita had already decided firmly that Lucia had the morals of a hopped-up alley cat.

But because Lucia had her sights centered on the same little house in Connecticut that Rita was thinking about.

She didn't like the way Phil looked at her either, she decided. He looked at her as though he wanted to devour her, and although his eyes never stayed in one place for any appreciable length of time, she kept catching them on her, judging her, appraising her, hungry for her.

It wasn't the sort of hunger that would lead to a house in Connecticut. It was the sort of hunger that would lead to a bedroom, and while Rita suspected that she would enjoy an hour in bed with Phil more than with Ned, sex was not her main goal at the moment.

She wished he would stop looking at her like that.

The party broke up a little after dawn. It was a Saturday and the two men didn't have to work that day, so they took the girls home on the subway and bought breakfast at an all-night cafeteria on

42nd Street. Then they walked to 47th Street, and then they said good-night all around, and then Rita went up to her room.

The shower felt good that morning. It drummed on her skin and sent needles of exhilarating pain through her firm flesh, and the smooth soap slithered pleasantly over her body. She washed her hair, deciding firmly that she would not cut it. Her hair always grew quickly; it was almost shoulder length already, and it wouldn't be too long before it trailed down her back.

She caught herself wondering whether Ned liked long hair.

She laughed, ducking back under the water and rinsing herself. Rubbing herself dry with the little towel, she went on thinking about Ned, about the kind of life she might be able to have with him.

It wasn't Golden Beach, of course. Unless he was unusually competent and unusually lucky she would never get to Golden Beach with him, but the possibility did exist. If he got a real break, if he could start an agency on his own and make a go of it then he could hit Golden Beach, or damned close to it. That was what he had told her, if not in those exact words. And she believed him.

What was Connecticut like? She pictured small, compact houses with rolling lawns and shrubbery, maybe a garden in the back and children playing on the back lawn. And a dog—she had always wanted a dog, but the dogs around the Flagler Street docks were mangy yellow things that died periodically of distemper and nosed in turned over garbage cans for food.

Flagler Street was no place for a dog—or for a human being, for that matter.

•   •   •

She slept well that day. She was growing more and more accustomed to sleeping days and staying up nights, and with the light out and the brick wall so close to her window it was not hard to sleep in the daytime.

She didn't wake up until three in the afternoon.

She woke up quickly, all at once, clambering easily out of bed and dressing quickly. She opened the window wider and stuck her head out to gulp fresh air, filling her lungs and feeling very much alive.

Then she noticed the letter that had been slipped under her door while she was sleeping.

It was from Pardo: more of the same—he loved her, he wanted her, she belonged to him, and on and on. This time she didn't bother to read it a second time or to walk the floor thinking about it. For just a single second the memory of Pardo's arms around her pressed in upon her mind, but it vanished almost at once.

She strode very deliberately to the window.

She tore the letter into a dozen pieces and watched them float downward into the alleyway.

CHAPTER 7

It had, of course, been only a question of time.

From the day Rita first started working at the Cinderella, she thought of moving out of the rooming house and taking an apartment in the Village with Lucia. For some reason which she couldn't fathom she never quite managed to suggest that move to the other girl, but when Lucia came up with the idea she was instantly in favor of it.

It made sense.

They moved on a Tuesday afternoon, because neither the Play Pen nor the Cinderella were open on Tuesday night. They packed their clothes and Lucia's pictures in their suitcases and took a taxi to the apartment on Horatio Street that Rita had picked out the previous afternoon, and once they were inside and their clothing put away Rita realized how much better an apartment was than a furnished room.

There was the kitchen, for one thing. It was small, with a two-burner gas stove and a midget refrigerator, but it was a kitchen she could cook in. It meant an end to breakfast in a greasy lunch counter and dinner in a restaurant she couldn't really afford.

She was saving money. She couldn't really help saving the money as the weeks passed. Finch was paying her $100 a week, the room was costing $8 and Danton was getting $10. And $82 a week was far more than she could spend. A minimum of $20 a week had been going into her savings account, with a high of $40 one week when she ate like a bird and went out for dinner with Ned several times.

So the apartment wasn't really one tremendous extravagance. It cost her and Lucia $45 a month each, but she saved on carfare and meals and wound up almost even on the deal. It meant an extra trip for Lucia, but since she and Phil had been doubling with Ned and Rita almost every night, she would have been coming down to the Village anyway.

It took only three days for Pardo to send a letter to the apartment.

She was used to his letters by now. She didn't open them any more, tossing them into the garbage can the minute she took them from the mailbox in the hallway. The first one that reached her in the new apartment she read, wondering how he had obtained her new address so quickly. But since then they landed in the garbage, unopened.

Her dates with Ned became increasingly more interesting every night. After they had been going together for a little over a week—without him even making a move to kiss her goodnight—he asked her if she would sleep with him.

Strangely, the question didn't shake her composure in the least. It came as a total surprise to her, but he put the question so naturally that she wasn't taken aback. She told him that she wouldn't, that she intended to wait until she was married, and he nodded and didn't press her further.

That night he kissed her.

Gradually he wanted more and more from her, although he never tried to get her into a bed. They would sit for hours in his apartment, kissing and holding one another. His hands would find her breasts and hold them gently, very gently, as if he was afraid to hurt her. His mouth was always soft and warm against hers even when he was insistent and demanding. She felt unbelievably comfortable nestled in his arms with the rest of the apartment dark and silent and the wind blowing outside.

He didn't excite her. She liked him, liked to be with him, liked to kiss him and touch him and to be kissed and touched by him. But there was never any acute physical hunger, never any craving for the raw animal contact she had had with Pardo.

She saw him every night.

And every morning Pardo's letters wound up in the garbage can.

Unopened.

It was just shy of a month after she and Lucia moved into the apartment on Horatio Street that Rita decided to get Annie Cross's job.

When she stopped to think about it afterwards it seemed very strange to her. She certainly had no desire to spend her life taking off her clothes, and she had no particular need for the extra $30 a week the specialty act paid. It was money, of course, and she could always find some use for money.

But at the time she had her mind busy with the notion of a home in Connecticut, and the money should have seemed quite insignificant. Logically, she should have stayed in the chorus until Ned married her—as she was quite sure he would eventually do.

Nonetheless from the minute she hit on a way to beat out Annie Cross she couldn't help trying. It was a spirit that had been burned into her on Flagler Street, the spirit of survival, the spirit of pushing upward. It was what kept some kids alive in slums while other kids who didn't have the spirit died. It was the same drive that made Ned and Phil fight their way upward on Madison Avenue.

She couldn't help it.

She built her routine up from the ground. She practiced in her room in front of her mirror, and she thought of practicing in front of Ned but was afraid to. Just watching herself in her mirror was enough to convince her that Ned—or any other man—would be uncontrollable after watching her dance. It wasn't her body, although that was undoubtedly a part of it.

It was the dance.

It took only ten days before the dance was perfect. She played a record of "Caravan" over and over until it wore out on the record player she picked up in a Third Avenue pawnshop, and when she was ready she marched into Jacob Finch's office on a Thursday afternoon with her shoulders back and a determined smile on her lips.

When he returned her glance she remembered that first day, the day on the office floor, the day he gave her a job in exchange for her body. But the smile stayed on her lips.

He blinked for a moment. "Oh," he said suddenly. "I didn't recognize you in that get-up and without your makeup. Whattaya want?"

"I want to replace Annie Cross," she said.

"Huh?"

She repeated her sentence.

He laughed. "You kidding? What in hell can you do to replace the twister?"

She didn't laugh. "I can up your take a good 50%," she said. "I can get more people in here than you can serve shellac to. I can make money for you, Mr. Finch."

"No cracks about the drinks or you're out on your ear."

"You watch my act and you won't throw me out," she said. "You'll let me pour your damned drinks on the floor if I feel like it. All you got to do is watch."

He shrugged. "So I'll watch. Go ahead—but if you're no good I might toss you out for the hell of it. Wise broads I need like a hole in my head."

"You mean like another hole in your head. You got one already."

"Listen—"

"Come on outside," she said. "Just watch me for a minute or two and you'll keep your mouth shut."

He didn't answer her. She walked out of the office and he stood up from his chair and followed her. She could feel his eyes on her body as she walked, and she knew that he was going to like her act. He couldn't help it.

"Get a piano player," she said. "I don't need a whole orchestra for this one, but I've got to have somebody making with the piano."

"She don't need a whole orchestra," Finch said to the ceiling. "She only needs a piano player. The New York Philharmonic I don't have to hire, on account of she don't need a whole orchestra but only—"

"Get me a piano player. I don't want to waste my time."

He started to say something but stopped. "Look," he said finally, "I can't dig up a piano player at this hour. You come barging in on me in the middle of the afternoon and you expect me to find a piano player. I should maybe turn over a stone and find a piano player under it?"

"I can play the piano, Mr. Finch."

He turned at the voice. It was the Negro janitor who swept the place every afternoon. He had been standing only a few feet from them, but he was so silent and moved so slowly both of them had forgotten he was there.

"You can?"

The Negro nodded.

"You know 'Caravan'?" Rita demanded.

He nodded again, his face devoid of expression. Finch motioned toward the piano and he sat down at the stool, playing a few chords and runs experimentally. His fingers moved deftly over the keys, and Rita was surprised that he could play so well. He was so old and moved so slowly that it seemed out of character for him.

"You ought to get this piano tuned, Mr. Finch," he said. "It's pretty bad."

"Nobody comes to listen to the music," Finch said. The Negro didn't answer.

Rita walked onto the stage. She was wearing an outfit that made her look about sixteen years old and had no makeup on her face.

"There's no makeup for a reason," she told Finch. "You'll see why in a minute. But I wanted you to know so you'll get the full picture."

"Just dance," he said. "Get the damned thing over with. Then I can fire you."

"You won't. And this is the costume I wear, just a skirt and blouse like this."

"It makes you look like a kid," he said.

"I know." She turned to the piano player. "Play 'Caravan,' please."

"Any special key?"

"Low," she said. "Sexy."

He began to play. She let him go on for sixteen bars while Finch regarded her with a bored what-the-hell expression. Then she began to dance.

Except it wasn't a dance exactly. Her feet moved in time to the music, but watching her you weren't conscious of the music at all, or of the fact that she was moving in time to anything at all. She danced around slowly, moving back and forth and tightening and relaxing the muscles in her shoulders. She shook her head from side to side and you could see the fear in her eyes, fear mingled with pure terror.

One hand went to her throat and stopped there. Her month opened and closed but no sound came out of it.

Then she unbuttoned the top button of her blouse.

Her hand dropped immediately and she took what appeared to be an involuntary step backward. She shook her head violently from side to side and mouthed "No" silently. She swayed with the music and breathed heavily.

Then she opened the next button.

One by one she opened the buttons of her blouse. When she was halfway done her perfect breasts were visible through the opening in the blouse and she heard Finch gasp audibly. She kept moving to the music, kept undressing more and more, kept shaking her head and maintained the expression of horror on her face.

When the blouse was completely unbuttoned she began to writhe and twist in the center of the stage like a woman on fire. She let out a little moan from deep down in her throat and her breasts heaved.

She parted the blouse completely, baring her breasts. She let the blouse drop slowly, very slowly from her shoulders. It fell to the floor and her eyes followed it to the ground.

She continued to move to the music. Dancing, her whole body dipping and swaying in a manner that was both awkward and graceful all at once, she began to cry. First she started to whimper. Then she sobbed.

"No," she said in a whisper. "No."

She stepped back. Then her hands found the zipper of the skirt and fumbled with it. She released the zipper, still keeping in perfect time to the music. She shook her head violently again, stepping back and saying "No" louder than before.

Then, after she took a deep breath and held it in her lungs without losing the insistent beat of the piano, she took the zipper between her thumb and forefinger and yanked it all the way down.

Beads of sweat covered the forehead of the Negro piano player. His eyes were not on the keys; he played without looking at the piano, hardly conscious of the keyboard beneath his fingers.

The veins stood out on Jacob Finch's forehead and his mouth hung open. He couldn't move.

All he could do was stare.

Jerking her hips from side to side, she shivered her way out of the skirt. It fell slowly, inching its way down over her full hips and thighs, down past her knees until it touched the floor. Her mouth fell open and she stepped out of the crumpled skirt and left it in a tired heap on the floor. She kicked at it, absently, and stepped backwards once again.

Now the expression of fear and agony on her face was almost painful to look at. Her eyes were wide and terrified. Her mouth was open and she seemed to be trying to say something but no words came from her lips.

She began to dance, faster. She was going in double time now and the Negro automatically increased the tempo of the music to match her speed without taking his eyes from her body. She whirled faster and faster.

Then, abruptly, she came to a complete stop and stared dully in front of her.

"*No*," she said. The word exploded from her lips.

"No!"

She started to cry again, her body once more taking up the unceasing rhythm of the music. Then her thumbs found the elastic band of the yellow panties and hooked themselves under it.

She let go of the elastic and shouted "NO!"

Then her thumbs found the elastic once more and tugged at it. The panties began to come down from her hips. She inched them further and further. She slipped out of them just as she slipped out of the skirt and kicked them away, standing entirely naked in the center of the stage.

"Please," she whispered. "Please!"

Again she stepped back one step. Her arms crossed in front of her bare breasts. At the same time she tried to cover herself with her hands.

"Please," she begged again.

Then her eyes closed and her mouth dropped open. Her arms fell limply to her sides. She was naked, open and defenseless.

She screamed "NOOOOOOO!" at the very top of her lungs, letting the single syllable end in a hideous, agonizingly painful shriek. Then, slowly, she fell backward until she lay absolutely motionless on the floor.

The club remained in complete silence for over a minute. A clock ticked somewhere in the back. The piano had stopped. Even the breathing of the trio was inaudible.

"Jesus Christ," Finch said.

The piano player didn't say anything. Rita stood up quickly and began pulling on her clothes.

"Jesus Christ," Finch repeated. "Rape."

Nobody said anything.

"Every man," he went on. "Every man in the audience'll be raping you. Every man in the audience'll be raping a virgin."

Rita smiled.

"That's why no makeup," he said. "That's why the school-girl outfit. I shoulda figured it."

He closed his eyes and shook his head slowly from side to side.

"I'd be wearing a flesh-colored G-string in the show," Rita said. "Of course."

Finch nodded.

"I want $150 a week."

"Annie's been getting $130," he said. "And she started at $120."

"I don't give a damn what Annie's been getting," she said levelly. "I want $150."

"$135," he suggested.

"You bargain with me," she said, "and you can take this rattrap of yours and stick it."

He looked at her and she looked back at him.

"I ought to ask for more," she said. "I'll make ten times that for you the first week, you son of a bitch."

He nodded. "Yeah," he said. "$150."

She turned suddenly to the piano player. "What's your name?" she asked.

"Ray," he said. "Ray Jenkins."

"He's going to accompany me," she said.

Finch said, "Wait a minute. I got a band hired as it is. I need another piano player like I need—"

"A girl named Rita Martin," she finished for him. "I want him."

"But—"

"Both or nothing," she said. "I'm not kidding."

He hesitated. "Okay," he said.

"You pay him union scale. No less."

He nodded.

"And no kickbacks."

He nodded again. "You start tonight," he said. "No more wasting you on the chorus. Okay?"

"All right. But you pay Annie for the whole week."

"I gotta," he said. "It's the rules."

She laughed. "Don't look so damned sad about it. You can afford it."

The funny part of it was that she certainly didn't need the extra $20. $130 would have been plenty, but she asked for the full sum without thinking twice.

Why?

Because I could get it, she answered herself instantly. If she could get something she had to take it. She had to grab all she could all the time, grab everything that came her way. It was the only way.

When she returned to the club that night Annie Cross's name was absent from the marquee and hers was on it instead. It stood out in three-inch letters directly under the name of the headliner, who that week happened to be a blonde Amazon named Marinda Keen. RITA "SCHOOLGIRL" MARTIN it said—and she had to laugh, thinking how true it was.

Because she was a schoolgirl. She could be at home right now, doing her homework, worrying about a date for the senior prom, helping her mother straighten up the room.

She laughed again, wondering how Finch would feel if he knew he was guilty of statutory rape. And she laughed once more, remembering that Ned too thought she was nineteen. How would he react if he knew he'd been dating a sixteen-year-old?

Inside the club Rita pushed both Finch and Ned from her mind. The other girls didn't talk to her, but this in itself was not strange. She had never bothered to develop friendships with them anyway.

But she could sense a definite feeling of hostility in the air. Perhaps most of it stemmed from jealousy—she made a break for herself while they remained in the chorus, and it wouldn't be strange for them to resent it. In addition, everybody who worked at the Cinderella liked Annie Cross.

And Annie Cross was now out of a job.

That, she decided, was life. Ray met her backstage, looking as tired as usual but much more alive in a dark flannel suit.

"You look nice, Miss Martin," he said. "You'll be good tonight."

She smiled. "I hope so."

"You will. No need to worry, Miss Martin."

"Call me Rita," she said.

"Sure, Rita. Thanks for getting me the job. Don't know why you did, but thanks."

"I like the way you play."

He shrugged.

"You play very well," she went on. "Especially after I was halfway through the act, when you stopped playing the melody and started fooling around with the chord structure. You play piano a lot, don't you?"

"On the weekends I do a bit uptown."

"What do you play mostly?"

"Modern stuff," he said. "Bud Powell-ish, Thelonius Monk-ish stuff. I'll have to be careful accompanying you, careful I don't get too far out."

"Don't worry about that."

"Have to," he said, smiling. "The squares don't want to hear music. They want a nice simple melody, something they don't have to listen very hard to understand. If I get far-out they won't dig it."

"Play it your way," she said. "They'll love it."

And they loved it. She knew they would, knew it from the second she stepped on the stage and the junglebeat of "Caravan" came up from the piano. She knew it the minute she started to move around the stage, knew it the first time she heard a slight gasp from the audience.

She knew it when the applause came loud and spontaneous and uncontrolled. They loved her.

Chapter 8

Phil Travis waved a hand in the air. "Another round," he called to the waiter. "Bring everybody another drink."

Ned said, "Phil, take it easy. We don't have to drink heavily here. There's a bottle in the apartment and we can—"

Phil silenced him. "This is my party," he insisted. "Soon as you get your break you can pay for the drinks. It's my turn now and I'm damned if I'll stop."

Phil was a little drunk, but Rita thought that he had a perfect right to be a little drunk—or even a great deal drunk, for that matter. It was Tuesday night, and that afternoon Joe Nester, one of the partners in the agency where Phil and Ned worked, had told Phil he wouldn't be toting mail from office to office anymore. He was getting a tryout in the copywriting department, and that meant he was on his way up.

Since Tuesday was a night off for the two girls, it seemed the obvious time for a party—and a party was definitely in order. Not only had Phil been promoted, but Lucia had landed a job in the chorus at the Cinderella to replace Rita. Both of them were pleased to be working in the same show, and if Lucia was jealous of the fact that Rita had better billing and was making better money, she wasn't letting it show.

The party started at the Dime Note, a small modern jazz club on Cooper Square that Ray Jenkins had recommended enthusiastically. Rita had grown very fond of Ray in the few weeks they'd been playing together, and had gotten into the habit of listening to him fooling around with the piano for a half-hour or so before the show each night.

Ray's playing, as he himself insisted, was not the greatest thing in the world. "It's too derivative," he told her. "I play like other guys play instead of thinking along fresh musical lines for myself. But it's a kick."

It definitely was a kick, and Rita discovered that modern jazz was her kind of music. There was a hard, tough quality to it—and it took a little concentration to "get the message." But it was her kind of message—deep and intense and gutsy, with a sort of bluesy, crying tone to it.

The music at the Dime Note was the same kind of music—"hard bop" Ray called it, and the term seemed to fit. There was a quarter playing there, with piano, bass, drums, and tenor saxophone. The club was small and quiet, with everybody listening steadily to the music and drinking somewhat expensive drinks.

The party started there, but it wasn't the sort of party that could stay all night at a quiet club. Phil felt like talking, so after two rounds of drinks the four of them took a cab to a noisier club on Fourth Street just off Sheridan, Dixieland, but they took a table in the rear where they could hear themselves talk without competing with the music.

Phil was very excited and very proud of himself. If someone else had been that proud of himself Rita would have called him— privately, at least — a conceited ass. But somehow Phil

Travis didn't fit her definition of the term. Phil was, somehow, too self-assured, too sure in his own mind of his own success to be conceited. Conceit, to Rita, seemed to imply some inner doubt submerged behind a facade of false assurance.

If Phil Travis acted conceited but couldn't be so, Ned wasn't conceited but could be. Phil held the spotlight that evening, but Ned occupied the major part of Rita's attention. She searched his face for some symptom of jealousy which deserved to be there, and was consequently puzzled when she couldn't find it.

He *seemed* to be enjoying Phil's success. This didn't make sense to Rita, and she was impatient to get him alone and figure him out more carefully. While she didn't want him to be so jealous as to ruin his future with it, she still didn't want him to be acquiescent, to relax and let Phil pass him by. In a strange sort of a way she felt as though she had an investment in Ned. She had already devoted plenty of time to him, time she could have spent with other men. Ned could be a part of her future; he could be the bulk of her future, for that matter.

She wanted to guard her investment.

Returning to the conversation, she picked up her drink and drained half of it. It was a Gibson—the ad man's drink, Phil called it. To Rita it was a martini with an onion replacing the traditional olive and the vermouth applied with an eyedropper.

But it was a very nice Gibson, and she thought that the other Gibsons had been very nice Gibsons indeed. In fact she was beginning to become very fond of Gibsons.

She was also becoming a little drunk, and enjoying the whole notion of becoming very drunk. She had never been very drunk, or even slightly drunk for that matter.

It was pleasant.

"See me during lunch," Phil was saying, repeating once again the conversation with Nester. "That's all he said, and when I saw the bastard after lunch he gave me a shit eating smile and said, 'I saw that copy you worked up for the Lawson promotion. Not bad.' Not bad, he called it. I busted my hump on it and he called it 'not bad.'"

"It wasn't bad," she heard Ned mumble to himself.

"Then he said, 'You can try writing some more copy. You'll be getting twenty bucks more a week. I think you'll work out.'"

It went on. Rita was glad for the Gibson—and for all the other little Gibsons that had preceded it. Sober, the night might have become a quietly horrible bore; drunk, it was pleasant and relaxing and even stimulating in a dizzy sort of a way. Drunk, Phil seemed to have just finished rocketing to the moon instead of having pulled in an additional $20 a week. Drunk, he was a conqueror who had an empire kneeling at his feet; sober, he would have been a nuisance.

"Let's get out of here," Phil said suddenly. "I'm sick of this place."

"Sure," Lucia said. "Where to next?" She stood up and reeled slightly.

"My place. I'm sick of these damned clubs." Phil stood up, covering the check with a bill and leading the four of them to the door. Rita followed with Ned.

"I think they want to be alone," Ned whispered to her. "He'll be taking her to our place. Okay with you if we go to your apartment for a little while?"

Rita nodded without answering. She wondered idly whether

Lucia would sleep with Phil. She hadn't so far, but tonight she might be drunk enough and pleased enough with his promotion to drop her resolution about holding out for a wedding.

And she talked enough about sex. Although Rita wasn't actually at the point where she needed a man, she was having more trouble dropping Pardo's letters in the wastebasket. She had even opened the last one, feeling a momentary thrill at his words on the sheet of paper.

It was the same sort of thing as the last one she had seen: he loved her, he could give her more than she could get even on $150 a week (he had learned about her work at the Cinderella) and on and on.

But Lucia seemed so sex-hungry! The books she read, the pictures on the walls, the conversation—it was a continual surprise to Rita that Lucia hadn't dragged Phil off to bed instead of it being the other way around.

At the corner of Seventh Avenue and Barrow Street the party split up. No goodbyes were said; Phil and Lucia turned silently toward the boys' apartment and Ned and Rita headed toward the Horatio Street apartment.

The night was cool—cool and crisp and as silent as a New York night ever gets. She could hear a subway train underground, rushing from Harlem to Flatbush Avenue. Cars passed by, windows in buildings opened or closed, people walked singly over the streets of the city. Once a boat whistle from the Hudson sounded loud and shrill, breaking as it did into what seemed like silence.

The buildings hid the sliver of moon; there were no stars. Ned's hand found hers automatically and held it, pressing it tightly from time to time as they walked. Then he released her hand and his arm slid quite naturally around her waist.

She felt comfortable.

Her body moved closer to his and she relaxed, letting herself lean just a little against his. Her head moved over and rested on his shoulder. For several blocks neither of them said a word.

"Tired?" he said finally.

"Not too. Drunk, I think."

"Yeah."

They passed a cop who walked slowly with a bored expression on his face. He was swinging a nightstick on a leather thong from his right hand, swinging it in a perfect and perfectly monotonous rhythm.

A bakery truck passed them. A doorway they passed revealed a boy and girl about Rita's age holding each other very close with their mouths pressed together.

"He deserved it," Ned said.

"Huh?"

"The promotion. He deserved it."

She didn't say anything.

"He's been doing good copy," Ned went on. "He's hot—he'll be good in the business."

"I suppose so."

He didn't seem to have heard her. "But I deserved it more. Hell, the son of a bitch got that break because of the Lawson account. Phil didn't do a goddam thing on the Lawson job. That was my work, every lousy word of it."

Her mouth fell open.

"Every lousy word," he repeated vaguely.

"Then—"

"Nester told him to give it a try. Phil didn't; he forgot and goofed around until the night it was due and then he had a date with Lucia. So he told me to do it for him and I did. And that's what got him the copywriting gig."

They went on in complete silence for half a block. Then she pulled away from him and stopped walking and looked straight into his eyes.

"Two things," she said. "One—don't ever tell anybody else in the world that Phil didn't write that copy."

He nodded. "And what's two?"

"Two is don't ever do a single piece of work for anybody else again or I'll break your arm."

He sat down on the couch and she went around the room turning the lights out very methodically and quickly. It was a ritual with them: he would sit down on the couch with a stack of records on the phonograph and she would turn off the lights. Then they would begin.

They began. She sat next to him and he pulled her close, his arms going around her body and pressing her to him. His mouth closed over hers and their lips met. He kissed her gently the first time; then he pressed his mouth hard against hers, harder than he usually did, and his tongue forced her lips apart and pushed itself between them.

He released her and lifted her head in his big hands, running the tip of his thumb over her chin. He kissed her, little quick kisses that covered her forehead and her eyelids. He kissed her cheeks and the tip of her nose; then his arms went around her again and their mouths met.

"I love you," he said.

It was the first time he had said that to her.

He kissed her again, more insistently than before. Their bodies moved slightly apart and his hand cupped her breast. He didn't squeeze it or move his hand at all but held it, almost protectively, almost tenderly.

"I love you," he said again. She didn't answer him.

He began unbuttoning the buttons of her dress. Her dress buttoned down the back and unbuttoning it was not especially subtle, but subtlety didn't seem particularly important at the moment. He unhooked the hook-and-eye arrangement at the top of the dress and it fell to her waist, freeing her breasts.

His hands took them and they were warm to his touch. For a moment neither of them moved; then she put her hands behind his head and pressed his face to her breasts. He kissed her breasts, one and then the other, and he pressed his hungry mouth against the firm white flesh of the valley between them. He kissed the nipple of one breast, thrilling her, and his tongue circled it and caressed it gently and tortuously.

"I love you," he said once again.

Hurriedly he struggled to pull the dress down over her hips. She wanted him all of a sudden, wanted him with her whole body. Half her mind knew that she didn't love him, that she would probably never love him, that he didn't even excite her as a lover.

But her mind seemed to have very little to say in the matter.

He pushed down her dress and her panties and stroked the hard flat stomach, pressing kisses against it and sending her pulse up another notch. She turned in her seat and stretched out on the couch and he kneeled over her, kissing her and touching her all over.

She thought, "No!" —and then she said the word, once, making it flat and extremely positive in the silence and closeness of the room. At first he didn't seem to have heard; she repeated the word louder and he fell back.

He turned his face to hers. The expression in his eyes was frighteningly desperate. "I . . . I have to," he told her. His voice was half croak and half whisper.

She closed her eyes and shook her head from side to side vigorously. "No," she repeated. "I . . . you know what I told you, Ned."

He was silent.

"I'm sorry," she added lamely. Her *body* was sorry, she realized, but her mind was almost triumphant.

Again he didn't answer for a moment, and when he did his eyes avoided hers. "Rita," he said, his voice strained and unreal. "Honey, it . . . hurts a man. I can't stop like this. It—it hurts to walk. It's bad for me."

She thought a moment. "Isn't there any way—?"

He smiled. "There's one hell of a good way. But you're holding out for a ring on your finger, remember?"

"I don't mean that. Isn't there any other way?"

He nodded without speaking. Carefully he rearranged her clothing, pulling up her panties but leaving her breasts bare. Then he lay down beside her, his mouth on hers and his body upon her.

He began to move against her. She was lost for a moment; then she moved with him, helping him. His breathing became very fast and his arms tightened around her and she became caught up in passion, not her passion but his.

She could hear his heart beating very quickly. She could feel him moving against her and the force of his excitement alone excited her. The entire process seemed to go on forever without taking any real time at all.

And then it happened for him. His body stiffened against hers, tight, hard, and then a tiny sob tore forth from his throat and he went limp in her arms. She held him very close, loving the way his head felt on her shoulder, loving the feeling of him so very close to her.

His breathing, unbelievably heavy, was the only sound she could hear. It filled the room.

They lay very still for several minutes.

"I love you," he said.

And then he said, "I want to marry you."

CHAPTER 9

"He wants to marry me," she said.

Lucia didn't answer. Lucia was in a strange mood, Rita thought. She had returned to the apartment with an almost blank stare in her eyes and she hadn't said a word, simply sitting up in the leather chair and looking across the room at the far wall. She had a cigarette between the second and third fingers of her right hand, but she didn't bother to drag on it. She held it motionless and the smoke drifted in a gray column to the ceiling.

"Of course I accepted," Rita continued. "I'd be a fool not to. He said he wanted to marry me right away and he couldn't stand waiting, but he would first have to get his first promotion. He said he doesn't want his wife to work."

"You'll still be working. So he makes seventy or eighty bucks a week? You'll still be taking home twice as much."

"I know," Rita said. "He knows all that, too. But the first promotion seems to mean a lot to him. I think he's pretty jealous of Phil."

Lucia seemed to wince slightly at the mention of the name, and Rita wondered just what had taken place at Phil's apartment.

"I don't blame him for being jealous," Lucia said suddenly. "Jealousy can be a very easy pit to fall in. I'm jealous, Rita. I'm jealous of you."

Rita's eyes widened but she managed to remain silent.

"Don't be surprised," Lucia went on listlessly. "Why the hell shouldn't I be jealous of you? I show you the ropes and give you an intro to my agent and you wind up in the same show with me with top billing. I set up a date for you and you wind up marrying that guy. I—"

"Wait a minute. You didn't want Ned, did you?"

"Of course not."

"Then—"

"Shut up, will you?"

Rita's mouth snapped shut and the room was silent again. Rita wanted to get up from her chair and go to bed, but somehow she couldn't move. She could tell that Lucia wanted to talk but didn't know where to start. She felt alternately close to the other girl and infinitely removed from her, and the evening both tightened the bond between them, creating an urgency for communication, and at the same time pushed them further apart.

She waited for Lucia to speak.

And after a few moments Lucia did speak, but when she did her voice seemed to be coming through a filter. There was no rise or fall to her voice—it was all the same tone, all the same monotonous and inflectionless patter. First Lucia put her cigarette out in the bronze ashtray; then she began talking.

"I didn't want Ned," she said. "But I wanted Phil. You probably can't understand how much I wanted him, but that doesn't matter. I figured we'd get married and I could get away from this damn rat race and have a couple kids and that.

"I don't love him. That's important, because it's a part of the rest of it. If he dropped dead tomorrow I wouldn't cry about it.

To me he's just another man, but I thought he might wind up marrying me.

"But he won't ever marry me, Rita."

"Why not?"

A pause. Then, "Because I let him lay me tonight."

Another pause. "I didn't want to, Rita. I didn't want to let him because I knew once he had me he wouldn't want to marry me. Hell, I've met guys like Phil Travis before. I've been laid by better men than him and I know what it's all about. I'm no little hick with sun in my eyes and hay on the back of my dress.

"And I knew he'd try to make me—hell, he's been trying since the day I met him. I gave him this song-and-dance about how he should put the ring on the finger first, and I used this nice round body of mine to work him into a lather every time I got near him.

"I thought I had him by the throat, Rita."

"But—"

"But I didn't." She shook her head impatiently. "I don't know why I'm bugging you with all this."

"It's all right. I don't mind."

Lucia nodded. "Sure. Well, we went to his place tonight. I knew he'd try tonight but I didn't care. I was pretty drunk, but I can't blame it on that. I could have stopped him if I wanted to."

"Why didn't you?"

She shrugged. "I don't know. The funny part of it is that I was never the least bit excited. You read in confession stories about the poor little girl who gets so excited that she doesn't know what's coming off. Hell, I knew what was coming off. First my dress was coming off and then my bra was coming off and next thing my pants were coming off. And I'll give you three guesses what happened after that."

"I only need one guess."

"Yeah. And so that was that. He didn't even have to give me any crap about how much he loved me. I suppose I could have held out for an 'I love you,' but I didn't even bother. I just stretched out on the bed and let the son of a bitch have his fun."

Another pause. "How . . . how was it?"

Lucia laughed. "The same as always."

"What does that mean?"

Lucia laughed again, bitterly. "You ever been with a man, honey?"

Rita hesitated, then nodded.

"How many men?"

"Two."

"Like it?"

"With one of them."

"Which was that? The dope who writes you all the time?"

Rita nodded.

"And it was good?"

She nodded again.

"You're one up on me, sugar. I've been banged by the best of 'em and I've never had the least kick from the whole routine. And Phil was the same as the rest—he may be one hell of a bedmate, but you couldn't prove it by little Lucia. I was bored stiff by the whole performance."

Rita didn't say anything. There didn't seem to be anything to say.

"The lady was unmoved. Totally unmoved. Oh, he loved the

whole bit—don't worry about that. I can be pretty hot stuff in the hay when I feel like it. It's a shame I don't get any kicks for myself."

"Then why did you—"

"Let him? Because the sonofabitch was so clever about it. Because maybe I expected to get excited. Oh, I don't know. You sleep around and each time you think this'll be the right time, and you like the guy a little when you're with him, and then it happens and it's no good again. I don't know."

"Wasn't it ever any good?"

Lucia shook her head. "Baby," she said, "little Lucia stopped being a virgin at age thirteen. Isn't that one for the books?"

She must have looked shocked, because Lucia added hurriedly, "And it wasn't any of little Lucia's fault. Little Lucia lived with her aunt and uncle, you see, because little Lucia's folks were both as dead as doornails by this time, and little Lucia's uncle was a man named Uncle Ben who drank like a fish, and I guess little Lucia's Aunt Rose evidently wasn't the best thing in the world between the sheets.

"So one fine spring day Uncle Ben came in smelling of cheap wine, and he came into little Lucia's little old bedroom where little Lucia was sleeping. And I'll give you three guesses what he did to little Lucia."

"Oh."

Lucia's curtain of composure fell. "It was terrible, baby. I woke up with my arms and legs pinned down and my uncle's breath coming at me full force. And he kept mumbling my name and pinching me and trying to kiss me, and then when he did it to me it hurt like hell and I screamed my lungs out and—

"And then Uncle Ben hit little Lucia in the teeth and little

Lucia was out cold for a few hours. And when little Lucia finally woke up neither she nor Uncle Ben ever said anything about the little old matter again. Nice, huh?"

"Why, that's awful!"

"Well, it was hardly my idea of the best way to bring up a kid. But—"

"How could you stand to live with him?"

She shrugged. "It wasn't that bad. He felt pretty rotten about it once he was sober and made me promise not to tell, and I got the lion's share of candy and a higher allowance from there on in."

"Did he ever try it again?"

"Never. I would have killed him if he did, and I think he knew it."

A few seconds later Lucia stood up. "I'm going to bed," she announced. "I'm happy for you, sugar. You keep holding out until Ned puts the ring on your finger and you'll be all right. And don't worry about me. Little Lucia will find another man in good time."

"Are you sure Phil won't marry you?"

"Positive—he's that kind of guy."

"Will you be seeing him any more?"

"Sure—it's something to do, anyway. And it's somebody to go to bed with when there's nothing else to do."

Ned must have worked like a demon, because it was only three weeks later that he got his promotion. He burst into her apartment at six one evening with his eyes shining.

"You're not working tonight," he said. "We're going to celebrate."

"Celebrate what?" she asked, although she knew instantly what he must have been talking about.

After he told her, they celebrated. They celebrated differently from before, by themselves and without Lucia and Phil. First they had dinner at Bertoni's, an unassuming but expensive steakhouse around the corner from her apartment.

Then they returned to her apartment.

"I don't want other people around," he told her. "We'll have enough of them at that party tomorrow night." The party was one given by friends of Ned's from the office.

"Then what do you want to do?"

"Talk," he said. "And make plans."

"Plans for what?" she teased.

"Plans for a wedding—and for a wedding night." He kissed her. "I'm looking forward to that wedding night."

"You are?"

"Umm-hmmm. Aren't you?"

"Oh, I guess so. A little."

He put his arm around her shoulder and drew her closer to him. His left hand cupped her breast. "Just a little?"

"A little."

"Not a lot?"

"Well—"

He kissed her again. His mouth bore down hard on hers and his tongue met hers. She returned his kiss, wondering to herself how she could remain so cold and dispassionate while he made love to her and she pretended to return that love.

"I love you," he said.

She told him that she loved him.

"And we're going to get married."

"When?" she asked, trying to keep her anxiety from showing in her voice.

"You in a hurry?"

"Uh-huh."

H squeezed her breast gently. "Much of a hurry?"

"Yep."

"What are you in a hurry for?"

"To be married."

"That's all?"

"Well..."

"Why wait?" he demanded suddenly. "Look, we can't get married until I get another raise. That'll be a month, maybe two."

"We could get married right now," she insisted. "I'm earning enough money so that—"

"When we get married," he cut in, "you won't be working any more."

"That's silly." They had argued about this before.

"It isn't silly. Rita, I don't want to sound stuffy, but I can't have a wife working in a strip joint while I'm trying to make it on Madison Avenue. Things just don't work that way. Don't you see?"

"But who would care?"

He shook his head impatiently. "Don't be a damned fool, Rita. Suppose a boss of mine walked in and saw you?"

"So what? How would he know who I was?"

"And then suppose he met you at a party. Baby, don't argue

with me, huh? We'll be married in two months at the most, but we can't get married until then."

She didn't say anything.

"Are you mad?"

She didn't answer.

"What's the matter, honey?"

"Nothing's the matter."

"What's troubling you? You can tell me."

"It's just . . . I don't know."

He waited for her to go on, while she looked for the right phrase.

"It's just that I hate to . . . hold out on you, Ned. I want to make love to you, too—but I don't want to do it until we're married."

"I know that."

"And at the same time I don't want you to think I'm teasing or anything, or just hungry to marry you. Can you understand?"

A smile spread over his face and he nestled his head against her breast.

"Don't worry," he said. "I understand, darling."

She let her own face relax into a smile. She could handle him, she knew. She wouldn't make the same mistake Lucia had made.

She could twist Ned Barnes around her little finger.

The party the next evening was uptown on the East Side in a re-modeled apartment in the eighties. The building was a run-down, almost ramshackle affair, and Rita was surprised when she got a look at the apartment. If not exactly plush, it was certainly furnished well and in excellent taste.

The apartment belonged to a man named Rustin, and Rita never did manage to catch his first name. Rustin and virtually everyone else at the party was connected in some way or other with advertising, although only Phil and Ned worked at Rosen and Nester, Inc.

Ned started drinking heavily right at the start. Everybody was busy congratulating him on his promotion, and while the congratulations had a phony ring to Rita's ears he didn't seem to notice anything. He drank one drink after another and laughed and joked with everybody.

At the start Rita tried to match him drink for drink. For one thing, she knew that there was nothing duller than being with a drinker and remaining sober yourself. In addition, she felt like getting an edge on.

That morning she had realized how much she needed a man. For a change she opened a letter from Pardo, and just reading his words was enough to restore the memory of his lovemaking. The memory didn't seem faded at all, and every detail of that one night was fixed and clear in her mind.

And, even though she didn't love Ned Barnes and didn't want to sleep with him, she was conscious of how much she needed to sleep with somebody. It was taking on the proportions of an acute physical desire, and she didn't like being in the position of wanting something that she was unable to obtain.

If only he would hurry up and get his silly raise so that they could be married! Last night she had even considered letting him take her, simply because she wanted it so much. But fortunately her mind had triumphed over her body. Perhaps he would still marry her even if she let him possess her before marriage.

Still, it was a chance she couldn't afford to take.

Why wouldn't he be sensible? They could be married immediately, and she could keep her job. Or, for that matter, she could quit her job and they could get by on his salary. She had enough money saved up to ride them over any rough spots. Her savings account grew every week, and it coupled with his salary would be enough to keep them alive.

It was his pride, she decided. He wanted to support her all by himself—and although she considered that sort of pride silly, it was something she could understand. If it weren't for that same type of pride she would never have come to New York herself.

At the same time, she was glad that Ned was proud. For the time being it meant a sacrifice, but in the future it would pay off. Pride and drive were prerequisites for success on Madison Avenue, and she hadn't the slightest desire to marry a failure.

It wasn't long before she gave up the attempt to match Ned drink for drink. For one thing, it became impossible. He was drinking very heavily, almost as though he wanted to lose control of himself and pass out. And she hadn't the slightest desire to pass out. The party itself was too interesting.

Lucia was in one corner, talking very earnestly to a little man with dark eyebrows and a very short crew cut. Another man—bald, fat and jowly—was sitting in the middle of the floor talking even more earnestly to himself. Ned was talking to whoever would listen, drinking whatever was handed to him and having himself a perfectly wonderful time, if she could judge from the inane grin on his face and the continuous patter of his conversation.

With a start Rita realized that she was actually quite bored.

The people at the party weren't her kind of people, and although she had picked up a good deal of background from Ned she still couldn't talk shop with all these ad-game people. They didn't talk her language, and the inside gags they laughed over went over her head for the most part.

She even caught herself wishing for a split-second that she was back on Flagler Street. Recognizing the thought, she forced it instantly from her mind.

It was a few minutes before midnight when Ned passed out. He wasn't messy about it in the least, pitching quietly over on his face without a word. Two of the men sat him up in a chair to let him sleep it off.

Rita studied him from across the room. There didn't seem to be anything in particular for her to do, so she just watched his face while he half-sat and half-sprawled in the chair. His eyes were closed; his breathing was free and regular.

A hand gripped her elbow. She turned slowly; it was Phil.

"Your man passed out," he said.

"I know."

"Come on into the next room," he said. "I want to talk to you."

Her mind spun slightly and she realized that the liquor was getting to her. "Wait a minute," she said. "Lucia—"

"Just passed out as cold as Ned did," he said. "So come on."

He propelled her through a doorway to another room and shut the door behind himself. The room was a bedroom and absolutely nothing else: the only piece of furniture in the room was a bed, and the bed literally filled the tiny room.

"What did you want to talk about?"

He sat down on the bed, patting the bedspread next to him. "Sit down," he said.

She looked around for someplace else to sit, not wanting to join him on the bed. But there were no chairs in the room.

He put his arm around her the second she sat down next to him. "Don't do that," she ordered.

He took his arm away.

She could feel weird sensations shooting through her body, and it only took her a moment to link those sensations with the night Pardo had made love to her. She wanted Phil Travis, wanted him badly—and the thought jolted her.

"What do you want to talk about?" she asked again.

He said, "I don't want to talk."

She took a breath and held it.

"You don't want to talk either," he said. "Do you?"

"I don't know what you're talking about."

He laughed out loud. "Come off it," he said. "You want it, don't you?"

She opened her mouth to say *no* but the word didn't come out. He took her in his arms, crushing her to him, and she wanted to push him away but couldn't.

Suddenly he released her. "Take your clothes off," he said. "Right now."

She looked at him dully, hating him. Then she stood up from the bed very deliberately and pulled her dress over her head. She stepped out of her panties; kicking off her shoes and reaching to unroll her stockings.

"Leave your stockings on," he commanded. "I like you better with them on."

She rolled them up again.

"Lie down on the bed," he ordered.

She stretched out on the bed. Her whole body seemed to have a will of its own and she was unable to follow what her mind was trying to tell her. It was unbelievable: he had hardly touched her, had only held her for the briefest moment in his arms.

Yet she was unable to do other than what he told her to do. His eyes burned into her and she followed out his orders, one after the other. He told her how to position her body on the bed, he told her to draw her legs apart, to bend them at the knee.

Then he laughed shortly. It was a harsh laugh, low and cruel.

"You want it," he said. "God, how you want it!"

She drew in her breath. He stood up and began removing his clothing, dropping it to the floor. Then, nude, he joined her on top of the bed.

He still didn't touch her.

"You handing Ned that line," he said. "And that clod believing it! Tell me how much you want it."

She closed her eyes. She wanted first to jump up and dress and leave him; next she wanted to grab him and pull him to her at once.

She waited.

"Bitch," he said. "What do you want me to do to you?"

She didn't answer.

"Tell me!"

She told him. She told him in words of one syllable, words of four letters each, words that she learned on Flagler Street. She had almost forgotten she knew those words but they poured free-ly from her lips.

Then he was upon her. His teeth sank into her shoulder in painful intensity and his body found hers. Their bodies joined in perfect rhythm, straining and grinding together, building higher and higher in pain and pleasure wrapped up inextricably.

She lost herself completely. She was overwhelmed, caught up in a brand new passion and glorying in the beauty and perfection of it. It seemed to her that it would last forever, that it would never end, that he would continue to make love to her as long as the world went around the sun.

On the crest of the final wave of passion it happened for them; then, suddenly it was over.

He stood up from the bed and looked down at her, the same cruel smile on his lips.

"A virgin," he said. "You actually had that sonofabitch Ned thinking you were a virgin."

She said, "Shut up."

"A virgin," he repeated, laughing. "No virgin ever had that cinder-shifting motion before, damn it!"

"Don't you ever tell him," she said shortly. "You ever tell him and I'll kill you."

Chapter 10

When she saw Ned the next night the first thought that came to her was that Phil had told him. She saw at once that something was wrong; he picked her up after her show and they walked half-way to her apartment in total silence. Twice she tried to get a conversation started but each time he let the conversation die out.

Something was wrong.

The apartment was empty. Lucia was with Phil, she knew; Lucia didn't seem to care any more whether or not Phil married her. He wouldn't marry her, and she knew he wouldn't marry her, but she slept with him anyway—even though she herself got no pleasure from it. Rita couldn't understand it.

Rita wondered vaguely whether Phil would tell Lucia what had happened the night before. He was the sort of man who would brag about what had happened, the sort of man who would delight in hurting one girl by boasting of the ease with which he had seduced another.

Would Lucia be angry?

But, she decided, Lucia didn't matter nearly so much as Ned did. And if he had told Ned . . .

She acted as if nothing had happened, waiting for him to make the first move. As usual they sat down on the couch, as usual he put his arms around her and kissed her, and as usual she returned his kiss.

Then he released her and looked at her. It was a long, searching look as if he was trying to probe her, to determine just what kind of a person she was.

"What's the matter?"

"Nothing," he said.

"Why are you looking at me like that?"

"It's nothing." He moved to kiss her but she dodged.

"Wait a minute," she said. "Ned, something's bothering you. Why not tell me about it?"

He took a deep breath and let the air out slowly. "Sure," he said. "Sure, I'll tell you."

He fumbled in his shirt pocket for a cigarette, offering her one automatically although he knew she didn't smoke. She refused the cigarette, lighting his for him and blowing out the match. She dropped the match in an ashtray.

He blew smoke at the ceiling. First he released a thin column of smoke. Then he blew smoke rings and his eyes followed them upward to the ceiling.

He looked at her again.

"Tell me," she said.

He hesitated. "Rita," he said. "Rita, there's something I have to ask you. If it's not true, I want you to tell me it's not true and to forget I ever asked you. If— The thing I'm worried about is that you'll hate me for thinking it might be true. Will you hate me, Rita?"

She forced herself to smile. "How can I answer that if I don't know what you're talking about?"

"I mean—I just don't want you to be mad for asking you."

"I won't be mad, Ned."

"Okay."

He drew again on the cigarette, expelling the smoke in a rush. "Rita, somebody told me some . . . things about you today. Now they probably aren't true. I don't believe them, baby. Or if they are true there's a reason . . . I mean—"

"Tell me what you heard," she said quietly. She felt that it must be about last night, that had to be what he was talking about, but he was certainly getting to it in a round-about way.

She couldn't make up her mind whether to deny the fact or to blame it on her drinking.

She waited for him to go on.

"Somebody told me," he began again. "Somebody said that . . . that your name is really Rita Morales and that you're a Cuban."

Then he stopped and looked away from her.

She closed her eyes. It was very strange—she hadn't expected that at all, and yet she was uncertain whether to be glad or not.

"Is that true?"

She hesitated.

"Is it?"

"Would it make a difference, Ned?"

"I don't know," he said honestly. "But I want to know."

"It's true," she said. "My name is Rita Morales. I suppose you could say I'm a Cuban, although I was born in this country—in Miami. I told you I came from Miami, Ned."

"Why didn't you tell me your real name?"

"Because that isn't my name any more."

"Why did you change it?"

"You don't get too far in New York with a name like Morales," she said. "I wouldn't have gotten work at the Cinderella if Finch knew I was a Cuban. Oh, if he found out now it wouldn't hurt me. He needs me now—but when he was hiring a chorus girl he could have lived without me.

"Ned, I paid two dollars a week less for that room on 47th Street because I signed in as Rita Martin. And if Tony Danton knew my real name I probably wouldn't have an agent right now."

"Why didn't you tell me?" he cut in. "I'm not your agent, for God's sake. I'm the guy who asked you to marry him."

"I didn't think it would make any difference to you, Ned. Does it?"

He didn't answer her question. "This . . . this guy who told me about your name. He told me something else, too."

"What?"

"About . . . about your mother."

She caught her breath. Her face fell, and she was glad he wasn't looking at her at the moment. "What did he tell you?" she asked.

"That she's a—"

"A whore," she supplied. "Don't be afraid to say the word, Ned."

"All right—a whore. That's what he said."

She closed her eyes. She could picture the house in Connecticut, the house with children playing in the yard. She could see now that she was never going to live in that house, never, and that everything she had been working for was going out the window.

"It's true," she said.

They sat together in silence. His arm still encircled her waist but it was numb and lifeless. Her whole body felt dead and distant, and she didn't think she could move if she had to. She wanted to die, to dig a hole and bury herself, to hold her breath forever so that she would die and everything would stop, just plain stop. She wanted to scream, to shout, to throw things.

Then he said, "Rita, why didn't you tell me?"

"Because I love you," she lied.

"That's why you didn't tell me?"

"Yes."

"I don't understand, Rita."

"You asked me to marry you," she said. "I . . . want to marry you, Ned. I want to be your wife. I . . . I was afraid that if you knew about my mother—"

"That I wouldn't want to marry you."

She nodded.

"Don't you think I have a right to know something like that?"

"Perhaps."

"Just perhaps?"

"I didn't think it would matter," she said. "You wouldn't be marrying my mother, Ned. You'd just be marrying me. It wouldn't matter what my family was."

"Are you so sure of that?"

She looked blank.

"Rita, don't you know that you can't live a lie? Don't you know that lies always catch up to you? Jesus Christ, use your head!"

"What are you talking about?"

He shook his head in exasperation. "Suppose we got married," he said. "Suppose I married you and we started to go places. I got a raise and another raise and maybe I start out on my own. Or Nester and Rosen take me in as a junior partner."

"That would be wonderful," she said.

"Of course it would. It's precisely what I'm aiming for. But suppose that happened and then *this* came out."

"You mean about my mother?"

"What the hell else could I mean?"

"Don't shout," she said. "How could it come out? How could anybody find out about it?"

"People always find out, Rita. People find out about everything. You could have figured that I wouldn't ever find out, either. But I did."

"So suppose they did find out," she said desperately. "What difference would it make, Ned? It wouldn't make that much of a difference."

"Wouldn't make a difference! It would kill my career, you idiot!"

She didn't say anything for several seconds. She thought, *I might hold him. I have to do this just right, but he still wants me. I haven't lost him yet.*

She said, "You said you loved me."

"I did."

"But you don't love me any more?"

"Of course I love you. I love you very much."

She hesitated. "You said you wanted to marry me."

"I did."

"And now?"

His mouth opened and his lips moved but he didn't say anything.

"Don't you want to marry me, Ned?"

"I—"

"I love you," she went on. "I love you very much, and I want to marry you. I think I would make a good wife for you, Ned."

"Rita—"

"Don't you want to marry me, Ned?"

"I . . . don't know."

"What do you love more?" she asked softly. "Me or the advertising business?"

"I don't *love* the business."

"You know what I mean. What do you love more—me or yourself?"

"Rita—"

"Won't you take a chance?"

"What do you mean?"

She was breathing heavily. "Won't you take a chance? Won't you chance your career? The odds are nobody will ever find out. Even if they do, they probably won't give a damn. So my mother's a whore—everybody'll think it's just some damned rumor. Nobody will believe it."

"They might believe it."

"They won't care enough about it. Oh, it'll keep you from ever being president of the United States. But you don't want to be president, do you?"

"No," he said. "Of course not."

"Well?" she demanded. "What *do* you want, Ned?"

"I'm not sure."

"Do you still want me to marry you?"

"I'm not sure of that either."

"What are you sure of, Ned?"

"I'm sure that I love you."

"Are you?"

He nodded.

She turned to him. She took his hand in hers and placed it on her breast. Then she placed his other hand under her skirt high up on her thigh.

"Hold me," she said.

He held her. Automatically his hands began to fondle her firm flesh and she knew that she had him hungry for her, wanting her.

"I love you," she told him.

His mouth moved toward hers. She moved away.

"Don't kiss me," she said. "I love you but I don't want you to kiss me."

"Why not?"

"Because I don't think you love me, Ned."

"You know I do."

"Do you still want me to marry you?"

"That's something I have to think about."

She pushed his hands away from her body and moved away from him on the couch. "Then you might as well go now," she said. "If you don't know now, you might as well go. I don't want to see you any more."

"Rita—"

"Go away," she said, hoping as she said it that he wouldn't go, hoping against hope that he would still want her enough to marry her.

"I won't go," he said.

She didn't say anything.

"I love you," he said. "I can't leave you. It would kill me to leave you."

"Then do you want to marry me?"

He said, "Yes," almost without a pause.

"Are you sure?"

"Yes."

She suppressed a small sigh of relief. "I'm glad," she said. "God, you don't know how glad I am. But I still want you to leave."

"Why?"

"I want you to be sure," she said. "I want you to think about it, Ned. I want you to tell me tomorrow whether you're sure that you want me. I don't want to use any unfair tricks to sway you."

Even as she said it she was pushing her tricks to the breaking point. She knew that only by sending him away could she secure him permanently, only by forcing him to make the decision by himself could she ensure his following through with that decision.

"You're a good woman," he said suddenly.

She smiled.

"You are," he said. "You really are. I already know what I want, Rita. I'll want the same thing tomorrow."

"Then go now. You can tell me tomorrow."

"And I'm not going to wait for that raise," he went on. "We'll be married next weekend, and we'll manage somehow. I know we can make it."

"Of course we can," she said. "That's what I've been telling you all along."

"It took tonight to make me see it. I . . . when I saw what it would be like not to have you, when I thought how it would be to give you up and never see you again . . . I don't want to waste any more time, Rita. I want to marry you right away."

"I love you," she said. She kissed him, then stood up from the couch. "You better go now," she said. "Pick me up at the club tomorrow night."

When he was gone she could hardly believe the whole thing had happened. They almost broke up; instead, they were going to get married right away. It was too perfect to be true, and she knew that she would have to thank Pardo for what he had done.

It had to be Pardo, she reasoned. No one else knew both that Carmen Morales was a prostitute and that Rita Martin was her daughter.

No one else would have told Ned, for that matter.

And so she was not at all surprised when the phone rang half an hour later and the voice on the other end of the line said, "*Buenos noches*, Rita."

"*Buenos noches*," she replied. "Good evening, Pardo."

"It is good to talk to you, Rita. When shall we go back to Miami?"

"I'm not going back to Miami, Pardo. You may go back whenever you wish. You may go back tonight, for all I care."

He chuckled. "Didn't your little advertising man talk to you this evening?"

"Yes," she said. "You are a bastard, Pardo."

He chuckled again. "And how are things between the two of you, Rita?"

"We're going to be married," she said. "This weekend."

There was no answer.

"Did you hear me, Pardo?"

"I heard you."

"Well?"

"He knows, and he will still marry you?"

"That's right."

He said, "You are very smart, Rita. He must love you very much."

"He does."

"And do you love him?"

"No—but he thinks I do."

"Why are you marrying him?"

She didn't answer.

"For money? I could buy him and sell him, Rita. I could have him killed or kill him myself. Why do you want him?"

She said softly, "You know why."

"Yes," he said. "Yes, I know. I will go back to Miami tonight, Rita. This is what you want, is it not?"

"Yes."

"I have missed you," he said. "You did not answer my letters."

"Of course not."

"I love you," he said. "But that does not matter."

"I wish you didn't," she said, honestly. "I wish you didn't love me or miss me."

"But I do. Wishing changes nothing."

"You will forget me."

"No," he said. "But you will forget your advertising person. You will want me."

"No."

"It is true," he said. "And I will always want you. You may come to me any time, Rita.

"I am not proud," he continued after a brief pause. "I will want you, no matter when you come to me.

"I will wait."

Chapter 11

Danton's bulk loomed at her across the desk. "Any other broad," he said, "would give her left tit for the chance I'm giving you."

"I know it," she said.

"$500 a week. You know what that adds up to a year?"

"Twenty-six thousand dollars."

"That's about it. You know how long it'll be before this dope of yours drags home that much?'"

"About ten years."

"If he's lucky. You know where you can go from here?"

"Where?"

"To the top," he said. "Straight to the goddamned top. You're out of your mind."

"I want to marry him."

"So marry him."

"I can't keep working and marry him."

He glared at her.

"I can't," she said. "Honest, Tony."

"Take the job," he advised. "Then you can buy him."

She sighed.

He took the cigarette from his mouth and ground it out. "Things come too damned easy to you," he said. "Too damned easy. First you twist Finch around on your finger. Then you get a shot at the top slot at Ruby's and you turn it down. What the hell's wrong with you?"

"I told you."

"You think I'm always going to be able to offer you work like this? What's wrong with you?"

"I can't take the job at Ruby's. And I can't keep on at the Cinderella."

"That's nice. Finch'll love you for that."

"To hell with Finch."

He laughed. "I've said the same thing myself dozens of times. But I hate to say to hell with Tony Danton."

She didn't answer.

"I could use the extra $2600 a year," he said. "No sense playing games. But I'm thinking of you, too."

"Sure—you're a philanthropist."

He didn't answer her, and she thought for a moment that she had hurt him.

"I'm sorry," she said. "I didn't mean that, Tony."

"Yeah."

"I—"

"Rita," he said, "it's not gonna work out. Every dame in the business figures to get out and marry some nice schmuck and live on a farm or something."

"Not a farm. A house in Connecticut."

"That's a farm," he said. "It's a goddamned farm with cities in it."

"It's what I want."

"Today it's what you want. A year from now you'll hate it."

"I don't think so."

"I do."

"Of course you do. You're wrong, but it's your life. You know, I could use that extra $2600."

"I know."

"You were a good client," he said. "You really were. No trouble, no backtalk—just plenty of work, plenty of money coming in. You ever decide to junk this schmuck, you look me up. Understand?"

All at once she felt very good. "I will," she said. "I hope I never want to, but if I do I'll know where to come."

He smiled.

"You're a good man," she said. "You try to be a bastard, but I think it's just an act."

"Get out," he said. "Get the hell out of here."

She got out. She got out and taxied back to her apartment, feeling for once very good and very happy. For all practical purposes, everything she worked for had been achieved. Flagler Street was a memory; soon it would be not even that. Golden Beach was still in the future but she was on the road to it already.

She had a man. Her man had a future, and she was a part of that future, and there was no more dancing at the Cinderella, no more rutting around on the ground with little men like Jacob Finch, no more of any of that sort of thing.

Back in her own apartment, with the taxi paid and tipped and the door shut behind her, the feeling of happiness persisted like the warm glow of a shot of brandy. She felt good inside, good and warm and secure.

Rita Barnes.

It was a nice name, she decided. Better than Rita Martin, far better than Rita Martino, and infinitely superior to Rita Morales.

It would be her name in a matter of days.

First there would be a blood test, then a waiting period of three days or so. Then there would be the wedding—a small civil ceremony with Ned and herself and a best man and a bridesmaid.

Lucia would be the bridesmaid, of course. And she supposed that Phil would be the best man, although she hoped inwardly that he would not. She didn't want to look at him again, because she knew that she could not look at him ever again without remembering that night at the party.

That terrible night.

But even with Phil as best man she could live through the wedding. And then they would go to a hotel room somewhere, she could guess, and then Ned would make love to her. She vowed to herself that she would make him happy.

It would be a slight problem, of course. She would have to act like a virgin and still be as good with him as she possibly could.

But she could manage it.

She stretched out on the couch like a large kitten, yawning and smiling contentedly. With her eyes closed she could picture the house in Connecticut perfectly. There would be a tree in front with leaves that were bright green in spring and summer and all colors of red and yellow in the fall. And at Christmas time there would be a pine tree in the living room with bulbs on it and presents under it, and a fire roaring in the fireplace.

She let her mind wander. She let her imagination have free

rein and she let her eyes remain closed, and the smile never disappeared from her lips.

She didn't even hear the door open.

His hands lifted her clear off the couch and hurled her at the wall. She was still asleep when he first touched her and she woke up to look at him as if she were coming out of a dream into a nightmare.

"You little bitch!"

It seemed like a nightmare. Ned's eyes were wild and red, his suit mussed and the expression on his face terrifying. She couldn't understand what was happening.

"Just like your mother," he shouted. He took a step toward her, his right hand balling into a fist.

"Just like your mother," he repeated.

"What are you talking about?" She could hardly get the words out.

"You know what I'm talking about. Don't try to give me that sweet-and-innocent act any more."

She could only shake her head in a mixture of wonder and fear.

"I know all about it," he said. "I know all about it, and the minute I found out I wanted to kill him. I went for him but he knocked me down, and thank God he did because he's the best friend I ever had."

He wasn't making any sense.

"What—"

"Shut up!"

She closed her mouth. He was about two feet away from her,

an insane light blazing in his eyes, and she hunched her body up against the wall in a vain attempt to get away from him. She couldn't understand it.

"So I left the apartment," he said. "I went out to get drunk, and I drank so much I got sick. But I couldn't get drunk! Do you understand that, you bitch? I couldn't get drunk! I couldn't stop remembering what he told me."

"What who told you?"

"Phil," he said, softly this time. "Phil told me."

And all at once she understood. All at once she knew what had happened, knew that the world she had built for herself was coming to an end. She opened her mouth to deny the charge but knew instinctively that it was no use.

Nothing was any use any more.

"I ought to kill you," he said. "I really ought to kill you. Do you know what I'm talking about."

She couldn't say anything.

"Driving me crazy," he said. "Hardly letting me touch you while you hold out for a ring and then you go screwing with my best friend. What kind of an animal are you?"

Her hands were trembling.

"I think I should kill you," he said. "How would you like that? I could break your goddamn bones one at a time and listen to you scream. Would you like that?"

"No," she whispered.

"You wouldn't? I think it might be fun. Come here!"

She pressed her back to the wall.

"Come here or I'll kill you." The statement was delivered flatly in an almost normal tone of voice. She had no doubt at all that he would kill her unless she did precisely as he told her.

When she stepped forward he hit her. His fist struck her in the chest over her heart and just below her breasts and knocked her back into the wall again. She could feel her heart pounding against her ribs and she thought for a moment that she was going to die.

And for a moment she almost wished for death, almost wished that he would beat her and kick her until it was all over for her so that nothing could harm her again, ever.

The hatred still burned in his eyes.

"Do you want me to kill you?"

"No," she said.

"Why not?"

She shook her head from side to side and her eyes were wide open with fear.

"Please," she said. "Please."

His hands dropped to his sides. "You would have married me," he said. "You almost did. If Phil hadn't told me, I would have wound up having you for a wife. You'd have been screwing for the whole neighborhood every day while I went to work. You would have . . ."

"No, no, I—"

"He almost didn't tell me," he went on. He didn't seem to notice her at all, talking as if she weren't even in the room. "He said he was going to tell me because it wasn't his business, but when I told him I was going to marry you he wouldn't hold back.

"He almost didn't tell me."

He slapped her. He slapped her with all his might and the

blow nearly knocked her head off. She fell to her knees, dazed, and when she stood up again and looked at him she saw that something had gone out of him.

He looked dead. She knew by looking at him that something was lost forever for him, that he would never be at all the same again. When he spoke his voice was very soft and almost like a machine.

"I'm not going to kill you," he said.

She was filled with relief. But she was still terribly afraid.

"I'm not going to kill you," he repeated. "All I'm going to do is get what I figure I got coming to me. That's all."

She couldn't understand what he was talking about. She closed her eyes for a moment, trying hysterically to picture the house in Connecticut, the house she would never live in.

Her mind was blank. All she could see was Flagler Street, with the children playing on the docks and the garbage and old newspapers littering the alleyway.

"You're just like your mother," he said. "Only your mother's better. At least she gets paid for it. You give it away, you dirty little tramp."

He smiled suddenly, but it wasn't a happy smile or even a smile of amusement. While he smiled his eyes remained perfectly expressionless.

"I'm going to get what I've been waiting for," he said. "Hell, you won't miss it. If I don't get it somebody else will, and I bet a hell of a lot of guys have had it from you already.

"You know what Phil called it? *That cinder-shifting motion.* He says you're pretty good in bed, Rita."

He stepped closer to her.

"I'm going to have my share," he said. "But first I'm going to fix you so you ache for a little while. I'm going to hurt you, Rita."

He hit her. His last blow had struck her in the chest, but this time his fist hit her lower, directly in the abdomen. The pain doubled her up and she almost got sick to her stomach.

Then he was dragging her away from the wall and into the center of the room. With one sweep of his hand he ripped her white blouse from her shoulders.

He hit her in the breast with his fist with all his strength. She sprawled full length on the floor, aching. The pain was greater than anything she had ever experienced before.

He took off her shoes, her skirt and her panties. Then he stood up, his face still devoid of expression, and began to remove the belt from his trousers.

Suddenly she knew what he was going to do.

"No!" she screamed.

The same dead smile appeared on his lips. "Just like in your act," he said. "Just like in that hot little dance you do at that whorehouse of a nightclub you work in. You let men think they're raping you, don't you?"

She couldn't say anything.

"It's real this time," he said, pulling the belt through the last loop. The belt was long and black, with a silver NB forming the buckle. He held it by the buckle and waved it experimentally in the air.

"Please," she said.

He smiled again.

"I'll do anything."

The smile grew wider. "You will," he said. "You'll do a great many things. But first there's something I have to do."

She could hear the sound of the belt whooshing through the air. Then she could neither hear nor see anything because the pain was tearing through her body. She wanted to scream but she couldn't even scream.

He whipped her very systematically. He first made her lie on her back, striking her across her breasts and belly and thighs. He didn't stop until every inch of her skin was red and sore from the beating.

Then he kicked her hard in the side and made her turn over on her stomach. She couldn't even shout now, couldn't even think of anything but the pain and agony. He brought the belt down across the backs of her legs, across her thighs and back, down on her shoulders.

She thought he would never stop.

When he kicked her again she rolled over automatically. He dropped the belt to the floor, pulling off his shirt and stepping out of his pants.

He knelt on the floor beside her and struck her again in the stomach with his fist.

He hit her again; then, unable to control himself any longer, he fell upon her and took her brutally, savagely, and horribly.

It was a long time before she could move. She lay on the floor, crying, her shoulders shaking. All of her body ached, and the pain was intensified by the knowledge that she had lost, that she had lost completely.

Not only the house in Connecticut.

She had lost Ned, and in losing him she had lost herself. She had worked and struggled to make the grade and she had managed to ruin everything in one night.

Finally she dragged herself to her feet. It was then that she noticed the two crisp dollar bills he had tossed to the floor beside her.

And then she began to cry again.

CHAPTER 12

That evening she drank herself to sleep. She drank Scotch, expensive Scotch, and she drank it straight from the bottle. Lucia didn't come home until after she had gone to sleep, so she was completely uninterrupted. Once there was a knock on the door but she ignored it; twice the telephone rang and each time she didn't bother to answer it.

It took almost the whole fifth of Scotch before she could sleep. She took her clothes and put them in the laundry bag. She drew a tub full off warm water and sat in it, letting the water draw the pain from her body. She dried herself gently with the soft towel, almost blotting the water rather than rubbing herself dry.

Her body ached all over.

Finally she sat nude on the edge of her little bed, the bottle of liquor in her hand. The first swallow she took didn't even taste particularly good, but it warmed her as it burned its way down to her stomach.

The second drink was better.

While she drank she listened to the voices. The voices were talking constantly to her, talking loud and clear from someplace in the center of her head. For awhile she thought that if she drank enough of the Scotch she could make the voices be still.

But the voices continued to talk.

These are not your people, one voice kept saying. *You do not belong here.*

And another voice said, *You're no good. You're a whore like your mother*.

Stop, she thought desperately. Shut up.

You can make it, a third voice insisted. It sounded like the voice of her schoolteacher—but it was so long since she had been to school, so long and so far away that she couldn't be sure.

Bad, said the second voice again. *You're bad.*

Another voice—was it her mother's?—said something in rapid-fire Spanish.

Bad, said the second voice. *Bad like your mother.*

Rita drank deeply. The bottle was almost empty and her head was swimming. She could hardly hear the voices any more, could barely make out what they were saying. She put the bottle on the floor by the side of her bed and slipped under the covers, resting her head on the pillow and letting her eyes close.

Bad, said the second voice. *Bad, bad, bad, bad, bad.*

The other voices were silent.

You were born to be bad, said the second voice.

She didn't even have a hangover when she woke up. Lucia had left the apartment, so when she opened her eyes she was still alone. Her head was clear and her eyes opened wide at once and she jumped out of bed.

She fried two eggs and boiled water for coffee. She ate the eggs without tasting them, drank the coffee without tasting it, dressed hardly knowing what clothes she was putting on.

It didn't seem to matter.

Then she pulled a chair over to the window and looked out of it, her eyes on the street. Horatio Street was thin and quiet. There were even a few trees for shade.

But she didn't even see anything when she looked out of the window.

She would have to call Tony, of course. He could find work for her, although it might be some time before he could locate an opening that she could fill. But there was almost five hundred dollars in her bank account and it would tide her through until a nightclub decided it needed a stripper.

She would survive.

She gritted her teeth momentarily, angry with herself that there was not more money in the bank. There would have been if she hadn't been spending money on clothes and if she had saved on small things.

But she hadn't expected this. Her mind reeled when she realized how close she had been to success. Now she was back where she had started from and she couldn't even start over.

Because Connecticut, she realized, had been an impossible dream. She was never going to marry someone like Ned, never going to have a little white house with green shutters or anything resembling it.

She could still be successful—but she would have to be successful in an altogether different way. When she got a job she would throw herself into the job wholeheartedly, working her best every minute of the day. She would dance her best and sleep with the right people—and step on whoever happened to get in her way.

This time, she decided firmly, no man was going to use her. There would be no Ned Barnes to make her reach for the moon and no Phil Travis to push the moon out of her reach.

This time there would be nobody but Rita Morales. This time nothing in the world would stop her.

Getting work wasn't that easy. A call to Tony revealed that, not only didn't he have anything new for her, but he could not get her back into the Cinderella.

"Finch got shut down," he explained. "The law decided to hit him for three yards a week and he wouldn't pay off. He's been giving them two hundred a week as is and he didn't want to cough up anymore.

"So they shut him down on some kind of a B-girl rap—help mingling with the customers and like that. Nothing that hasn't been going on all along and that they haven't known about, but cops make their own laws. He won't be open for thirty days."

So that ended that—and, needless to say, that left Lucia similarly unemployed. Lucia wasn't the thrifty sort, spending her money on whatever struck her fancy and never banking a cent of it. Rita's five hundred dollar bank account had to support the two of them.

The weeks passed.

The weeks passed slowly and monotonously, with the same deadly routine every day. Rita woke up every morning about ten, showered and dressed, cooked breakfast and ate breakfast, and called Tony Danton. Tony Danton then assured her in a most sympathetic tone that there was no work for her, telling her that he might have something for her any day.

Then she would read or walk. Sometimes she took long walks, roaming all over the Village and sometimes covering half of Manhattan in the course of a day.

But most of the time she read. At first she bought second-hand paperback books at two for a quarter from a used bookstore on Seventh Avenue and Bleecker Street. Then she discovered the library and borrowed books at no charge, reading book after book and barely remembering what she had read at all. Her eyes raced over the pages, letting her escape and lose herself in them.

Then there was dinner. She hardly talked to Lucia, because the older girl seemed to be living in a world all her own. She and Phil had broken up finally and completely and Lucia wasn't dating anyone any more. Lucia generally woke up after Rita had left the house and disappeared, returning only at dinner and leaving shortly thereafter.

Rita didn't know where she went and didn't care any more. She didn't care about anything, regarding those weeks as a part of her life that was going to be totally wasted out of sheer necessity.

As soon as she got a job she could begin to live again. As soon as Tony found her some work she could set her sights on a goal and get moving in that direction.

Until then, all she could do was waste her time as easily and painlessly as possible.

But the routine became unbearable. It was at its worst in the evenings. Then she would finish dinner and wash the dishes in the sink, drying them quickly with the dishcloth and putting them away in the cupboard. She would wipe the table with a damp rag and hang the rag on a peg over the sink, and she would wash whatever clothing she had worn the day before and hang it in the bathroom to dry.

This was easy enough. It was simple and mechanical, and on days like this she didn't mind simple and mechanical tasks. It was when there was nothing to do that she felt she was going out of her mind.

She could only read so much. Then there came a point where her eyes refused to focus on the book and it fell from her hand. Sometimes she would stare for hours at a spot on the wall, unable to close her eyes or to move her body from its position in the chair. Sometimes she walked back and forth in the apartment like a caged lion at a zoo—anxious to go somewhere, but having no place to go and nothing to do.

Those were the bad nights.

There was no way to cope with the bad nights. If she went for a walk it did nothing but remind her how alone she was and how little she had to do. If she went to a bar for a drink one of two things happened: either a man made a pass at her, in which case she had to leave and go back to her apartment, or no man made a pass at her, in which case she felt lonelier than ever and unwanted.

She couldn't win, not on the bad nights.

On the bad nights the voices came, too. The voices said the same things every time, but the voice that stood out loudest and clearest and the voice that did the most talking was the second voice.

You're bad, it told her, over and over. *You're no good.*

In a way the voices were almost like company for her. When she was alone she could listen to them, could even answer them if she wanted to. Some nights she would hold long conversations with the voices; one night, seated by herself on a bench in Washington Square Park, she started talking out loud to the voices. Only when a man stopped to stare at her did she realize that the voices were not really there.

You're like your mother, the second voice said. *You were born to be bad.*

It was on one of the bad nights that Lucia walked into the apartment early—about nine or a few minutes after. She walked through the door with a blank expression on her face, her pocketbook dangling from one arm.

"Here," she said.

She threw three ten-dollar bills in Rita's lap.

"What's this for?"

"Money," Lucia said vacantly. "You've been paying all the bills this past little while. My turn."

"Where did you get it?"

Lucia collapsed into a chair. "Worked," she said.

"You've got a job?"

Lucia laughed, and her laughter sounded hollow. "Yeah," she said. "Yeah, I got a job."

"Doing what?"

Lucia dipped into her pocketbook once and came out with a small white envelope. She tossed it to Rita.

"Here," she said. "Have a look for yourself."

There were four pictures in the envelope. In each of the

pictures there were a man and a woman, both naked, in a variety of interesting poses.

"But—"

"Take another look," Lucia suggested.

Rita turned to the pictures and drew in her breath sharply. The woman in the pictures was Lucia.

"Why?" she asked.

Lucia shrugged. "I'm sick of it," she said. "I'm fed up to here with doing nothing every goddamned day. There's this photographer a few blocks from here who makes a few extra bucks doing this sort of junk. I asked him if he could use a model. He could, so that was that."

"Who . . . who's the man in the pictures?"

"How the hell should I know? I just saw him tonight and I don't care if I never see him again."

Rita didn't say anything.

"Do you think what I did was wrong?"

"I don't know."

"I was just so sick of it," Lucia said. "I just couldn't take it any more, not earning a cent and just laying around all day. You know what I mean?"

Rita nodded. She knew.

"He didn't even do anything to me," she continued. "I thought it would be like . . . like whoring, you know? But it wasn't. I mean, we just got in position and Joe snapped the camera or whatever they do and that was that. He didn't lay me, is what I mean."

Rita studied the pictures. "He didn't?"

Lucia shook her head.

Rita returned the pictures to the envelope and passed them

to Lucia. "Here," she said. "If you want to put them on the wall, feel free."

Lucia put the envelope in her purse. For a long moment neither of them said anything, sitting silently in the room. Rita felt an idea forming in the back of her head. She closed her eyes, trying to concentrate. There was something about the pictures that had given her an idea.

"I talked to Joe after," Lucia said. "He said he can use me a couple times a week. That'll give us an extra sixty bucks or so, Rita."

"Don't go unless you want to. We still have enough money for a few weeks or so. Then we can start worrying."

"I don't mind it."

Silence.

The idea took shape. Rita stood up suddenly. "I want to meet your friend Joe," she announced.

Lucia's jaw fell. "You want to ... pose?"

"Nothing like that, exactly. I've just got a sort of an idea. I want to meet him."

"Any time you want."

"Tomorrow okay?"

"Fine," Lucia said. "He sleeps late; we'll go over to his pad about one."

Rita met Joe the next day. He was in his late thirties, a man who had tried to make the grade as a fashion photographer and who never quite got where he was going. He drank too much, wasted too much time, and wound up earning a precarious living taking passport photos, an occasional wedding picture, and periodically snapping some pornographic photos. Joe listened with his face blank while she explained what she had in mind.

"Okay," he said when she had finished. "I'll go along with you. It shouldn't be much trouble at all."

She made the phone call that night. She dialed the number and he answered after the second ring, his voice cool and relaxed over the phone.

"This is Rita," she said. "Rita Martin."

"Hello," he said, the surprise evident in his voice. "What do you want?"

"I want to see you."

"I—"

"I want you to sleep with me," she said. "Don't you want to?"

Silence.

"Don't you want to?"

"Of course I do," he said. "I thought ..."

"You thought I'd be angry?"

"Something like that."

"I'm not," she said. "All I know is that I want you. I want you right away."

She heard him chuckling. "You're a real animal, aren't you? Haven't you been getting much lately?"

"I didn't call you to get insulted," she said. "If you don't want to—"

"But I do," he insisted. "You're a hot one, little Rita. You want to come over here?"

"No," she said. "I don't want to chance meeting anybody that I wouldn't want to meet."

He laughed again. "Want me to come over there?"

"No."

"Well—"

"I borrowed a friend's apartment," she said. "It's at 76 Thompson Street. Do you know where that is?"

"Thompson—that's two blocks west of Macdougal?"

"That's right."

"Okay," he said. "When do you want me to come?"

"Now," she said. "It's apartment 3-C."

She heard his laughter filter through the receiver. "You sure are a hot one," he said. "Can't wait, can you?"

"No," she said. "No, I can't wait." She smiled softly to herself and replaced the receiver on the phone. Then she sat down on a chair and waited for him.

It didn't take him long. In less than ten minutes there was a knock on the door. She stood up and walked to the door and opened it.

He walked inside, taking off his suit jacket and tossing it carelessly on the chair. "I couldn't figure it," he said. "I thought I'd be on your shitlist."

"I just wanted you," she said. She was beginning to enjoy herself, watching the way he fumbled around. She began to feel strong, superior to him.

"The reason I told Ned," he said. "It's not that I had anything against you."

"I know."

"You wouldn't have been happy together," he said. "Hell, he's a straight kind of a guy. Hasn't been around women too much."

She didn't answer.

"That's why I told him. That's the only reason. Hell, it's not that I didn't think you're good enough for him. You're as good as he is any day of the week. In several respects he's something of a jerk, if you know what I mean."

"I know."

"Well," he said. "I just wanted you to know there was nothing personal in it."

Sure, she thought. *I just had a nice back for you to slip a knife in.* And she said, "I know."

"Well," he said.

"Come on—what are you waiting for?"

The smile of assurance returned to his lips. He reached for her and put his arms around her, pressing his mouth to hers. She returned his kiss, forcing her tongue between his lips and moving her hands over his back.

She led him to the bed. She made him sit down while she removed all her clothing; then she let him take her in his arms. His fingers closed around her breast and he kissed her again, more forcefully than before. Then she had him undress and lie down beside her.

He was breathing very rapidly, and she was amazed at the total detachment that filled her. She felt nothing, nothing whatsoever. She was neither excited nor disgusted. She hated him, hated him more than she had ever hated anybody before—yet she could not even feel revulsion toward the man.

She was merely bored.

He caressed her skillfully, touching her here and there, kissing her all over and moving his hard lean body against hers. Throughout the whole performance she was able to observe him with clinical disinterest, faking the proper responses while feeling nothing. His hands on her body were no more exciting than were her own hands when she washed herself.

She almost laughed once, thinking *It's like taking a bath without soap or water*.

He was panting, anxious to take her. Skillfully she pitched his passion higher and still higher, kissing his lips and eyes, stroking his thighs and murmuring his name over and over. His hands were all over her body and she knew that nothing could stop him now, that he wanted her so much he would never be able to control himself.

She wondered for a second whether this was the way her mother felt when she went to bed with a man for money. She guessed that it was the same sort of feeling, the same total lack of excitement and lack of emotion.

Born to be bad, the second voice told her. *A whore like your mother*.

She wrapped her arms around him suddenly and drew him down to her. He took her swiftly and passionately, repeating her name in a throaty whisper. She feigned orgasm at the exact instant of his climax, noticing how his shoulders trembled for a second and then how absolutely still and serene he seemed as he lay inert in her arms.

Born to be bad, the voice told her.

But she didn't feel bad at all.

There was a smile on Joe's face. "Perfect," he said. "First time I ever shot infrared film and it came out perfectly. Want a look?"

He moved aside and let her examine the prints. At first she

was jarred by the pictures of herself and Phil Travis—the act itself had been simple enough, but the proof of the act was almost shocking.

"They're good pictures," she said.

"Thanks."

"Awfully good," she said. "How could you get such good shots? I thought you have to stay absolutely motionless when you're posing for a picture."

He laughed. "You ever see sports shots in a newspaper?"

"Of course."

"Hell, you don't think they got guys who'll stand in mid-air with a basketball in their hands, do you? It's no tough bit to take a picture of something in motion. All you do is use a fast film and shoot with a fast shutter-speed. It's simple."

"Even when it's dark?"

"Generally you just use a flash," he said. "With something like this when you don't want a visible flash, you use infrared film and an infrared flash bulb. It makes a sound, though. Did you hear the bulbs popping?"

"I didn't hear a thing."

"That's good. I'm willing to bet the guy didn't hear 'em, then. He wouldn't a heard a cannon if you shot it off in the next room. He was kind of wrapped up in what he was doing, if you know what I mean."

She almost blushed. For some reason she didn't want to talk about it, even though she had been completely numb emotionally while she and Phil made love.

"How much do I owe you?" she asked.

"Nothing."

"Don't be silly," she said. "You've got some money coming for this. I can afford to pay you."

"You don't owe me a thing, Rita. For one thing, I can make a few bucks selling the pics. Besides, it was a hell of a good show you put on."

This time she came even closer to blushing. "Forget it about the show," she said. "And you can't sell the pictures."

"Why not?"

"Because I don't want my face all over 42nd Street."

"Huh?"

"I don't want anyone to recognize me," she said. "My face shows up pretty clearly in those shots."

"So what? Rita, after I retouch those pics nobody in the world could prove it's your face."

"Retouch them?"

"Natch. Some of the dolls who model for me are models. Other are dolls like Lucia—chorus babes and actresses down on their luck who want to pick up a quick piece of change. They don't want their faces smeared over the street either. All I gotta do is play with the negative a little and you couldn't pick 'em out of a crowd."

"But that picture Lucia showed me," she said. "It looked just like Lucia."

"That's just an unretouched shot. She wanted a set as a souvenir, but the ones that go on the market won't look anything like that."

"I see."

"So I'll make my pile from the pictures," he went on. "So you don't owe me anything."

She nodded. "I'd like about half-a-dozen unretouched prints of each shot," she said. "Before you fix the negative."

"Okay."

"And don't retouch his face," she said. "I think it'll be kind of funny having Phil Travis's face under the counter of every bookstore on 42nd Street."

"That's a good one," he said, chuckling. "You're okay, Rita."

She sat down on the bed and waited for him. It took less than a half hour for him to print up a batch of the pictures and dry them for her. He brought them to her in a large manila envelope.

"Here," he said. "Good luck, kid."

She took the pictures and started to go. Then at the doorway she turned. "Joe," she said, "you must get sort of worked up watching things like this."

"What do you mean?"

"You know—like watching me and Phil."

He shrugged. "I get used to it."

"Doesn't it make you . . . well, want to go to bed with me?"

His eyes narrowed. "I told you there was no charge for it. Get out of here, will you?"

"Maybe I don't want to get out."

"What in hell *do* you want?"

"Maybe I want to stay for awhile."

"Why would you want to go to bed with me?"

"Maybe I like you," she said.

"Sure."

"I do like you, Joe."

"You don't have to go to bed with everybody you like, do you?"

"Maybe I want to get the taste of Phil Travis out of my mouth. Does that make sense?"

"Maybe."

She didn't want him, not really. But she wanted a man, a man who wanted her, a man she didn't hate. She went to him with a smile on her face and her arms spread wide, went to him with her body warm for him.

He took her on the same bed that she and Phil had made love on. He made love to her, and while his caresses were not nearly as practiced as Phil's they were far more exciting, far more meaningful.

At one point she said, "I love you," even though she didn't love him and he knew she didn't. It made everything better somehow, better and fuller.

And then they reached climax together and she was holding him in her arms, holding him in the same position she had held Phil, and he was warm and still and soft against her.

She was relaxed at last, fully relaxed. She kissed him once, lazily and sleepily.

Then she slept.

CHAPTER 13

"You rotten tramp," he said. He handed the pictures back to her.

"You can keep them," she said. "I have more."

"I can't believe it," he said. "And to think Ned almost married you. God, what a cheap little whore you are!"

They were in his apartment. He was sitting on the bed and she was sitting in a chair a few feet away from him.

She was enjoying herself.

"I don't know what you expect to get from all this," he said. "If I had a wife and kids you could probably take me to the cleaners, but unfortunately, I don't. You can keep your damned pictures, Rita."

She smiled.

"Get the hell out of here," he said. "And don't call me again, huh? You want to get laid, you drag some bum in off the streets from here on. That's about all you deserve anyway."

"You're going to pay through the nose," she said. "You're going to pay for these pictures, Phil."

"Like hell I am.'

"You are—half of each week's salary."

He laughed. "When I start paying you $45 a week for those that'll be the day. Give me one reason why I shouldn't toss you out of here on your hot little rear, Rita."

"Just one reason?"

"One'll do."

She took a breath. "I'm sixteen years old," she said.

His jaw fell.

"Sixteen years old," she repeated. "You know what that means, Phil? That means I'm jail bait. San Quentin quail. That means you can go to jail for twenty years for these pictures."

His mouth opened but no words came out.

"Sixteen years old," she repeated.

He said, "I don't believe you, Rita. I don't believe a word of it."

"You better believe it. Twenty years is a long time."

"It's impossible."

"It's very possible. And it happens to be true."

"But how—"

"I'm pretty mature for my age," she said. "Didn't your buddy tell you? My mother's a Cuban whore from the docks in Miami. You grow up fast down there."

"But you worked at the Cinderella."

"So I bought a cabaret card," she said. "That wasn't too hard. But on the birth certificate it says I'm sixteen now, Phil. Do you still want me to get the hell out of here? Because if you do, I'll get the hell to a police station and you'll get the hell into jail. Is that what you want?"

He shook his head.

"$45 a week," she said. "Half your salary."

"For how long?"

"Forever. And when your salary goes up you can pay me half of whatever it is. When you make $20,000 a year, I'll be making $10,000."

"You're crazy."

"Sure," she said. "You tell me how crazy I am."

"You couldn't prove it," he said.

"Look at the pictures and tell me I couldn't prove it. Are you nuts, Phil?"

His hands were shaking. "No judge in the world would believe it," he said. "It's obviously arranged. You had to have somebody to take the pictures and you had to be willing to go along with the whole thing."

"So what?"

"Also you've been had by other guys. I'll get half a dozen people to swear they've been in the hay with you fifty times each."

"Go ahead. The law says it's the same no matter what."

"No jury would convict me," he said. "You're nothing but a little whore's daughter. I'd get off."

She smiled slowly and confidently.

"What are you smiling about?"

"If you want," she said, "we can go to court over the whole thing. You think you'd get off?"

"Of course."

"And what would you do for a living?"

He looked blank.

"You don't think you'd stay with your ad agency, do you? Not for a minute, Phil. Not for a minute. I'd drag your name into the papers and keep it there. You'd be one of the hottest little scandals in Manhattan by the time I got through with you. Do you want that?"

His face fell.

"You'd never get a job in this city again, Phil. You wouldn't be able to wash dishes on the Bowery by the time you won your case. Oh, you'd win—but it would be a fairly costly victory. Do you still want me to go?"

He didn't answer her.

She stood up and started for the door. "Wait," he said, hoarsely. "Don't go."

She turned around with a smile on her face.

"Don't go," he repeated.

"Half of whatever you make, Phil. For the rest of your life."

"Maybe we can make a deal," he began.

"No deals. You just heard my price."

He shook his head. "That's impossible."

"That's the way it's going to be."

"It's impossible," he repeated.

"$45 a week," she said. "When you get raised to $100, then you can start paying me $50. And so on all the way up."

"I could give you a pile," he said. "I could pay you off all in one lump sum and get rid of you."

"No good."

"Why not? Hell, do you have to bleed me to death a little at a time? I've got money saved. I could give you a couple thousand now if you'd just leave me alone."

She said, "That's not the way I want it."

"Why not?"

"It just isn't."

"Why? *For God's sake, why?*"

The smile disappeared from her face and her lips tightened into a thin line. "I'll tell you," she said. "I'll tell you, Phil. It's like this. You see, I was going to marry Ned. I was going to marry him, and you've probably managed to figure out that I didn't love him. But that didn't matter.

"He loved me. He loved me and he wanted to marry me just as much as I wanted to marry him. I would have been good for him, Phil. I would have made a good wife. And in spite of the fact that you managed to make love to me when I was drunk, I would have been faithful to him.

"I would have been good for him because I wanted to be his wife. I wanted to wind up in a little house in Connecticut with a big backyard and a couple kids. That's what I wanted, Phil. I wanted to have a man working to get to the top and I wanted to help my man along.

"I almost had it."

She took a breath and let it out slowly, fighting to keep herself from shouting.

"I almost had it," she went on. "Then you had to louse it up for me. You ruined it for both of us, Phil. If you had just managed to keep your damned mouth shut Ned and I would have been married.

"And when we were married, Ned and I would have shared everything. But that's all finished now. So you and I can share everything, Phil. We'll split your paycheck 50-50, every goddamned week for the rest of your life."

He said, "You've got me over a barrel, Rita."

"You deserve it."

"Maybe. Maybe I do."

He pulled a cigarette from the pack in his shirt pocket and

lighted it. He took a deep drag and held the smoke in his lungs for a long time, releasing it slowly.

"There has to be another way," he said.

"There isn't."

"I could kill you," he said. "Or have you killed."

"That wouldn't do you any good, Phil. I've read enough mystery stories. I have an envelope with the pictures and a letter that will go to the police if anything happens to me. So you wouldn't want anything to happen to me, would you?"

"I could kill myself," he suggested.

"You wouldn't do that. You're not the suicidal type, Phil. Not you."

"No," he said. "No, I guess I'm not. Rita, there has to be another way. You can't stick me in a pickle like this."

The thought came to her suddenly, out of the blue. She hadn't even considered it before and she couldn't believe it at first. For a long time she sat thinking about it, thinking over the possibility while he sat tense and nervous on the bed.

"There may be another way," she said slowly.

"Let's hear it."

"I don't think you'll like it. But it's the only other possibility."

"What is it?"

She said, "You could marry me."

"You're crazy."

"I didn't think you would want to. But that's the only other way."

"Why . . . why would you want to marry me? It doesn't make any sense, for God's sake. It doesn't make the slightest bit of sense."

"Not to you," she said. "It makes sense to me."

"How?"

"Can't you figure it out?"

He shook his head.

"I wanted Ned," she said. "If I can't have Ned I'll take you. And if I can't take you I'll settle for half your money. But it's up to you to decide."

He said, "I don't believe it."

"You don't seem to believe anything."

"Jesus," he said. "What kind of a woman are you?"

"I don't know," she said. "I really don't know. I'm a sixteen-year-old girl, Phil. I was born sixteen years ago, so that must be something. And sometimes I feel as though I've been living for about thirty years.

"I told you what I want. I'd be a good wife for you, believe it or not. I'd help you and I'd push you the way a woman is supposed to push her man. I'd be a good mother, too."

"Would you?" His eyes were flat and expressionless.

"I think so. And I'm good in bed, Phil. But you already know that."

"You should be. You've got the background for it."

"I'm good in bed," she said again. "But I wouldn't cheat on you, Phil—if you didn't want me to. And I'd let you do whatever you wanted. You could keep half the whores in New York in business and it wouldn't bother me."

He smiled involuntarily. "You make yourself sound like the perfect wife."

"I'd *be* the perfect wife."

"Why?" he asked. "Why you?"

"Because it's what I want. Can't you understand that? It's what I want."

"You'll do anything to get what you want, won't you?"

"Of course," she said. "You're the same way. You got out of the mailroom and into copywriting by stealing Ned's work, didn't you?"

"Did he tell you that?"

"He didn't tell me you stole it. I don't think he was clever enough to figure it out by himself."

"I guess not." He looked at her. "You're pretty sharp, Rita. Very sharp."

"I have to be."

He nodded.

"It's up to you," she said. "I've got you over a barrel and we both know it. You can play it any way you want. You can pay me half your salary for the rest of your life or you can marry me. It's all up to you, Phil. You take your choice and you pay your money."

He considered. "It'll be cheaper marrying you," he said. "That way at least I can file a joint tax return and—" He broke off suddenly. "Christ," he said, "this is ridiculous!"

"Maybe."

"It's insane," he said. "You're sixteen years old."

"You should have thought about that when you took me to bed."

"But you don't look sixteen."

"No," she said, "and I don't act sixteen."

"You don't."

The conversation stopped again. Unsure of herself, she got up from the chair and sat next to him on the bed. She was beginning to realize something about him, something she had half-known all along but that she had never admitted to herself before.

He was her kind of man.

She still didn't like him. She didn't hate him, at least not nearly so much as she had, but she didn't like him. He was her kind of man, but he wasn't a good man.

Still, she thought, she wasn't a particularly good sort of girl.

"I don't love you," she said suddenly. "I could probably convince you that I did, but I don't."

"That's not hard to see."

"But I could," she said. "That's the funny thing. I liked Ned very much and I don't like you at all, but I could love you maybe. I couldn't ever have loved Ned. Do you know what I'm getting at?"

"I think so."

"Make up your mind," she said. "Do you want to marry me?"

"No."

"Then—"

"Hang on. I don't want to marry you, but I don't want to pay you blackmail either. I have to choose one or the other, don't I?"

She took his hand in hers.

"I'll choose the wedding ring," he said. "It's probably the wrong choice, but it might be a good deal cheaper from the financial standpoint. And the other alternative is completely impossible."

"Then you'll marry me?"

"Yes," he said. "I guess this is a rather unique proposal."

"Yes," she said. "It is."

•   •   •

They were married on a Saturday morning. They were married by a civil clerk in city hall with two men pulled in off the street for witnesses, and when the diamond ring was on her finger Rita was not particularly excited or happy or even emotionally moved.

She felt as though she had arrived somewhere, and that was all.

They moved at once into an apartment in the eighties off Central Park. While they did not love each other, they both made love expertly, and this was adequate compensation for love as far as Rita was concerned. Every morning they woke up and she cooked breakfast; then Phil went to work and she straightened the house and read. Evenings he came home and she cooked dinner for him. Sometimes they went out to a show or movie; most of the time they stayed home together.

Phil advanced quickly at Nester and Rosen. He was burning with ambition, more so than before. It was as if he had to prove himself both to Rita and to himself, and he attacked his work with a vengeance. His salary rose proportionately, and both he and Rita recognized that their marriage was certainly not doing his work any harm.

And Rita knew that she had chosen a man who was good for her.

Sometimes the voice bothered her. There was only one voice now, the one that told her how bad she was. *You're a whore like your mother*, it would say over and over.

But she learned to ignore it.

When they had been married for almost two years she had a child, a boy. She had an easy time during pregnancy and the child she gave birth to was a healthy one.

She named him Louis. She named him after Pardo, Luis Felipe Pardo—although of course she didn't tell Phil this. This made her days even better; before she often felt alone when Phil went to the office, but now she had little Louis to look after.

It was the baby that made her love Phil. The child looked exactly like his father and she had loved the child even before its birth. When she felt it kicking inside her, when she saw how her belly had grown full and round with it, she couldn't help loving it.

And during her pregnancy Phil had fallen in love with her. He would rest his head upon her stomach to listen to the baby and he would tell her how wonderful she was, how much he needed her.

That was the beginning.

The time passed. There were more promotions for Phil until they did finally move to Connecticut. They bought a small home in Westport and Phil took an early train to the city every morning. Louis began to grow up and went to school; Rita joined the PTA and played bridge every Tuesday afternoon with a group of the women who lived in the same neighborhood. Bit by bit she settled down in the role of Rita Travis, wife of Philip Travis and mother of Louis Travis. Bit by bit all of Flagler Street and all of the Cinderella wore away, leaving only a few scars and some small memories.

She never thought of her family, except for an occasional thought of her mother when the voice reminded her. The voice, naturally, never stopped talking to her. But she began to think that even if the voice did stop she would go on hearing it.

The voice had become a habit.

She didn't see the few friends she had had in New York. Lucia drifted downhill gradually, never able to face reality and never able to get back on her feet again. Rita ran into her once on the street and hardly recognized her. She had been drinking steadily; she had probably been earning her living in a horizontal position, Rita guessed, judging from the clothes she wore and the gaudy makeup on her face.

She hadn't known the girls at the Cinderella well enough to care about them or to recognize them if she met them on the street. Finch she neither saw again nor cared about; he remained at his cheap strip joint and stayed stuck in his niche forever. Ray Jenkins died, she read one day in the newspaper. She was sorry; he had been a good man.

She passed Tony Danton once on the street on a shopping trip to Manhattan. He was as big as ever and looked prosperous, but he didn't recognize her and she didn't bother to say hello. While she had liked him, he was a part of her life that was over with.

She never saw Pardo and never received word from him. She never got any news of her family in Miami and didn't care about them in the least.

She had her dream.

And that was enough.

My Newsletter: I get out an email newsletter at unpredictable intervals, but rarely more often than every other week. I'll be happy to add you to the distribution list. A blank email to lawbloc@gmail.com with "newsletter" in the subject line will get you on the list, and a click of the "Unsubscribe" link will get you off it, should you ultimately decide you're happier without it.

Lawrence Block has been writing award-winning mystery and suspense fiction for half a century. You can read his thoughts about crime fiction and crime writers in *The Crime of Our Lives*, where this MWA Grand Master tells it straight. His most recent novels are *The Girl With the Deep Blue Eyes*; *The Burglar Who Counted the Spoons*, featuring Bernie Rhodenbarr; *Hit Me,* featuring Keller; and *A Drop of the Hard Stuff,* featuring Matthew Scudder, played by Liam Neeson in the film *A Walk Among the Tombstones.* Several of his other books have been filmed, although not terribly well. He's well known for his books for writers, including the classic *Telling Lies for Fun &f Profit,* and *The Liar's Bible.* In addition to prose works, he has written episodic television (*Tilt!*) and the Wong Kar-wai film, *My Blueberry Nights.* He is a modest and humble fellow, although you would never guess as much from this biographical note.

Email: lawbloc@gmail.com
Twitter: @LawrenceBlock
Facebook: lawrence.block
Website: lawrenceblock.com